DASHING
THROUGH
Christmas

A Christmas Creek Romance #8

Rachelle Ayala
Lovely Hearts Press

>>><<<

Christmas Creek Romance Series

Deck the Hearts, #1

Her Christmas Chance, #2

A Christmas Creek Carol, #3

Kitty, It's Cold Outside, #4

A Christmas Creek Caper, #5

Toy Soldier Christmas, #6

Red's Christmas Woodsman, #7

Dashing Through Christmas, #8

Dottie's Christmas Wish, #9

Chapter One

I'm late. I'm late. I'M LATE!!!

"Sorry, Mom, no time to talk. I'm so late!" Misty Jolly hung up the phone and ran out the door of the apartment she shared with her twin sister, Merry. Although they were identical, with matching sky-blue eyes and sandy-brown curls, Misty, who called herself an event planner, was always in a hurry while Merry enjoyed leisurely strolls between mailboxes, delivering mail and gossip in their hometown of Christmas Creek.

Christmas is a big deal, indeed the only deal their town celebrated year-round, all thanks to her grandfather, Nick the First, who was a set designer in Hollywood before retiring to a once sleepy lumber town named Gills Gulch. He transformed the town into a tourist destination for celebrating Christmas—in December, in January, February, and yes, in July.

Now, she, Misty Jolly, one of the younger Jolly daughters, had the chance to work for Christmas Creek's biggest tycoon—Gordon Gills the Fifth—who'd tasked her with the very important transformation of Southside Glen, the new luxury retail, entertainment, and hospitality center into a Winter Wonderland of Christmas glory.

In fact, he was texting her, and she was pulling on her gloves and fumbling for her keys.

Where are you? Gordon texted. *The contractor is waiting for you. He charges by the hour, and time is money.*

OMW, she abbreviated "on my way" and jumped into the Jeep she shared with her sister. Mom always worried about her driving the backroads to Southside Glen, but she couldn't waste time at the many stoplights dotting the streets in town as well as the inevitable traffic jam in front of the town square.

Hanging a sharp turn, she flew to the outskirts and wound her way through the foothills. The roads hadn't been plowed, and she briefly wondered whether she should have taken the snowmobile. But she wasn't sure whether she'd filled up the tank since her last jaunt, so she powered on, wheels spinning around the twists and turns.

Her cell phone rang and went straight to the Jeep's speaker via Bluetooth. She hit the accept call button. "Dad, I'm driving. Can't talk."

"We got you a hands-free device for this very reason," her father groused. "Doesn't Gordon know a blizzard is incoming? No contractors will be working under such conditions."

"The work is indoors. It's all underneath the convention center roof, remember?"

"Yes, and that's what's bothering all of us. Seems wrong to have the tree lighting indoors and fake snow brought in when we have the real deal outside." Her father, Nick Jolly the Second, had followed in his father's footsteps as an animatronics expert in Hollywood, only to have his skills obsoleted by computer graphics before coming home to Christmas Creek to raise his large family.

"Haven't you read the weather reports?" Misty fishtailed around a fallen log. "Having all the festivities under the roof of the convention center is safer and climate controlled. We won't have to deal with blizzards or freezing rain canceling Christmas caroling, and the children waiting to see Santa won't freeze their tushies off if the temperature drops."

"It just doesn't feel real, sweetie. But I understand. Gordon invested a lot of money into the hotel and convention center, not to mention all of the retail space he needs to lease year-round."

"This project has to succeed," Misty said, encouraged by her father's acknowledgment of the town's shaky finances. "I'm sure some of the tourist crowd will overflow to the Main Street businesses and the seasonal merchants will stay on to the new year."

"Maybe," her father conceded. "You haven't been to any of our traditional activities. We missed you at the gift wrapping party, and caroling is not the same without your soprano voice hitting the high notes."

"You have Merry to carry the tune," Misty said. "I'll try to be home for dinner."

Truth to tell, she had no spare time ever since she pitched the idea for the Christmas Extravaganza to Gordon—not that she wanted her family to know. They would view it as a betrayal of the town traditions Grandpa started—all that wassailing, sleigh riding, tree trimming, and snow people contests—outdoors, rain, sleet, snow, or shine, would be duplicated indoors under the convention center dome.

"Come early," Dad insisted. "Your mom is baking Christmas cookies, and you know how she loves having all her girls around for the frosting and decorating."

"I'll try." Her phone beeped with an incoming call. "Someone's calling me. Gotta go."

"I thought you'd be here five minutes ago," Gordon said. "Nate's threatening to call it a day. He says you didn't leave explicit instructions on how large the pens should be for the petting zoo and the pet adoption center, and he says the heater for Santa's throne will interfere with the snow blowing machine. Oh, and Mr. Weston's on his way. I told him not to come, but apparently word got out we're late. Very late and over budget. The ice-grooming machines need to be repaired, and the hay bales for the sock hop are moldy due to that leak under the skylights you failed to catch last inspection."

"Wait. Back up." Misty interrupted Gordon's tirade of complaints. "Mr. Weston isn't supposed to show up until Christmas Eve. Doesn't he have other properties to examine?"

"That marketing video you made went viral, and all of our rooms and vacation properties are booked solid. That spate of riots late summer and property damage in the large cities has made our neck of the woods *the* Christmas vacation destination across the country. Some of the tourists are trickling in early. Mr. Weston wants to have two Christmas Eves and two Christmas Days to accommodate the crowd. Maybe three each."

The Jeep hit a slick spot of ice coasting down Hill Road. Misty struggled with the steering and held her breath. It continued to slide sideways, but fortunately no one else was out on the roads. The wind whipped snow off an overhanging branch, briefly blinding her before the wiper blades could scatter the white stuff, and she found herself spun one hundred eighty degrees in the middle of the road.

"You still there?" Gordon asked.

"Yes, hit some ice, but I'm okay. I don't get how we can have two or three Christmas Eves and Christmas Days," she said when she caught her breath.

"Simple. We package the Christmas experience for the different groups of people depending on their dates of stay. We'll have the exact same schedule so no one will miss out. If we do three-day sprints, we can have December 20 through 22 for one group, December 23 through 25 would of course be the most expensive package, and then December 26 through 28 can be combined with Boxing Day and Kwanzaa celebrations."

"This is so unexpected," Misty said. "I'm not sure we can get everything ready. Besides, how will all of this interfere with the traditional events? There's the high school Christmas prom, the Christmas romance reading with the hunks, the mahjong tournament, the bake sale and candy making, and don't forget, we only have one Gala Ball at your mansion."

"We can do all of that at Southside Glen. The hotel has a ballroom bigger than my mansion, and I'm sure the restaurants would love to have caroling minstrels going table to table. The Christmas hunks musical chairs or laps can be done at the food court; the mahjong tournament can be under the northern lights display; the bake sale and those old-time farm activities can be done at the petting zoo. Don't forget we'll have a tree rivaling the Rockefeller Center underneath the stained-glass dome. It'll be surrounded by the ice-skating rink. There will be miniature train rides, reindeers to pet, the Christmas test kitchen, and the international Christmas food court. Many more attractions than the town square."

"I know all that. Who do you think contracted all the additional vendors and characters?"

"Better deliver," Gordon growled. "And the weather's not looking good."

"Oh, no!" Misty cried out at the road-closed barricade blocking the snowed-over road. "They didn't plow Sill Road and they blocked it off."

"Can't you get around the roadblock?" Gordon asked. "You have a Jeep."

"I don't have a strong man to help me pull the logs," she said.

"Go over them. You have to get over there before Mr. Weston arrives. You don't know what Nasty Nate will tell him or take the chance he'll raise his bids now that he knows the big guy is breathing down our necks."

"Is he flying in this weather? I doubt they'd let him land." Misty swished the wiper blades to full speed. "The snow's blowing horizontal."

"You don't know Dash Weston like I do," Gordon said. "If you guys thought I was a Grinch, he's a way darker shade of green than I ever was. All he cares about is green, and with the money he's losing from all the looting and property damage elsewhere, he's placing all his chips on us."

Dash Weston sounded like an ass, but he wasn't Misty's concern. Gordon was the one to do the schmoozing and business deals and making sure Mr. Weston didn't pull out. Gordon had gone all-in on Southside Glen and he'd mortgaged his mansion and all the property he'd inherited from his great-aunt, Miss Marney Gills, to make it happen.

"Don't worry. I've got this." She gritted her teeth. "We'll squeeze in three Christmas Extravaganza Experiences."

"If anyone can do it, it's Misty Jolly's Premiere Events. Just think of the name recognition you'll get if you pull this off. They'll have you planning royal weddings and presidential inaugurations by next year. I won't even get the pleasure of a callback."

"Ah, Gordie, you'll always be first on my list. As long as you're good to Holly. Gotta go. I can't get around the road block, so I have to take the detour. It's going to loop me all the way back around the airport."

"Just cut across the runway," Gordon said. "No one's flying in this weather."

"Okie doke." She hung up, shaking her head. Gordon was her older sister Holly's beau, and while he was one pushy dude, he was practically family since Holly moved into his mansion after his first Gala Ball when his father shot the chandelier and spent Christmas in jail.

Three Christmas Extravaganza Experiences coming up, including three Gala Balls—make that four. She was sure Holly would insist on the traditional one at the Gills Mansion with Dad and Mom presiding as Santa and Mrs. Claus and her brothers working the animatronics, sound system, and light shows. The theme this year was a Very Western Christmas, and she was all prepared to go as a showgirl. Now she would need three more costumes from her repertoire as sugar plum fairy, ice sprite, dancing doll, or frost ballerina.

She could do this.

She was a Jolly, after all. The entire Jolly family did Christmas, and no one did Christmas event planning better than Misty Jolly, soon to be planner of the stars and maybe a president or a princess. A girl could dream. Couldn't she?

Chapter Two

"I'm in a rush," Dash Weston, CEO of Weston International, said with one finger over his earpiece, ready to disconnect the call. His nosy Aunt Sharky was on the line, and he was desperate to escape her clutches, especially her elaborate Christmas dinners and incessant delving into his nonexistent personal life.

"Promise me you'll come by Christmas Day. I know my brother's working you to the bone, and I ought to knock some sense into his bonehead. I can't stand by and see you following in his footsteps."

"You know how hard it is in retail these days. If we don't make money over Christmas, we're done for. People aren't going out shopping like they used to. Most people are watching Christmas on TV instead of going out and doing things. Theme parks are closing and cruise ships are half-empty. Destination vacations are the biggest moneymakers, but only if we can deliver a truly immersive and authentic experience. Problem is all the rioting and looting has destroyed our usual theme parks, and foot traffic is down in the big cities where our flagship stores were burned down."

"Then take a break," Aunt Sharky said. "Can't do much when you're fighting a trend. People are homebodies these days. It's all about family and not going out in a crowd of strangers."

"I don't want to debate, but I really have to go."

"Where?" His stalwart aunt, his father's older sister, was not going to be put off so easily.

"One of our most promising developments is in Christmas Creek. It's a town that celebrates Christmas year-round. We're turning it into a destination vacation experience. An entire convention center devoted to everything Christmas. In a few days you can experience a lifetime of Christmas goodness. It's designed to be so addicting and fulfilling that you'll be coming back all the time. Did I tell you they celebrate Christmas year-round?"

"You don't even like Christmas!"

"You're right, but I need the green it brings in. You ought to spend Christmas in Christmas Creek this year."

"Out in that doohickey town? No, thank you. It's high time you stopped chasing your tail and settle down. When was the last time you went on a date?"

Not even his mother, who was estranged from his father and not speaking to him because Dash worked closely with his dad, asked him such personal questions.

"Aunt Sharky, I know you mean well, but I'm too busy to date. I really have to go."

"Where?" she asked again.

"Christmas Creek, and I have to get in before the blizzard shuts down the airport."

"Egads, boy!" Aunt Sharky snapped. "You're going to get yourself killed puddle jumping that crop duster of yours. Call me when you get in. I don't want to be worrying about you when I've got pie crusts to roll out, cookies to bake, tea cakes to frost, and peppermint bark to chill."

"I'll give you a call if their cell phone towers are still up."

"Good. You tell that brother of mine to get his head out of his ass and come to Christmas dinner. You hear? You make money on Christmas, and you owe it to the Christmas gods to pay homage."

"*If* we make money," he said. "Catch you later."

He flicked his earpiece in time to pick up another call. It was Gordon Gills, the CEO of the Christmas Creek project that he bet his retail empire on.

"Mr. Weston. There's a blizzard forecasted for this area." Gordon sounded suspiciously subdued. "You might be better off sitting this one out."

"I might, and I might not," Dash replied. In his line of work, it was always better to keep everyone on their toes. "Are we having problems?"

"Nothing we don't have under control," Gordon said. "It's just that my event planner has a full agenda, and she can't take time out of her day to show you around. The contractors need supervising, and there are a million details to hammer out."

"I won't be in her way," Dash said. "In fact, she doesn't need to know I'm there."

"But I'll know, and I would be tripping over everything by taking you around."

"You need not worry. I can take care of myself plenty."

"The airport might be closed, and the roads impassable."

"Which would be horrendous bad luck, don't you think?" Dash scowled at himself in his bathroom mirror. He'd nicked a spot on his neck while shaving and a trickle of blood oozed. "If the airport is closed and the roads are impassable, then how are the visitors going to arrive? If we get hit by a ton of cancellations, we're done for. Belly up."

"The weather is supposed to clear by the eighteenth," Gordon said. "I thought over what you said earlier, and I think we can squeeze in three full-fledged Christmas Extravaganza Experiences. That is, if the weather clears and the roads are open."

"This is a risk I didn't foresee." Dash dabbed at his shaving cut. Oh well, he'd cover it with a red silk cravat. "Better start praying to the Christmas gods."

"Shall I meet you at the airport?" Gordon asked.

"No need," Dash said. "You won't know if I'm among you."

"Why the mystery? Why won't you show your face? You're our biggest investor."

"I like it that way. Perhaps Dash Weston isn't my real name either," he suggested, knowing that the reason Weston International was so impeccably managed was because of their army of mystery tourists, including his father and all the women he dated and enlisted to be mystery shoppers.

"I'll be looking for you," Gordon said to no avail, mainly because he didn't know *what* to look for.

Dash's face was never shown on any company reports, and neither was his father's, Aunt Sharky's, or any of his father's many lady friends. His mother might have outed them long ago, but hefty dividend payments bought her silence. Whenever they went on video conferencing calls, they used avatars. His father was a whale shark and he was a hammerhead shark. Aunt Sharky preferred the great white with her big mouth wide open, and his sister and assistant, Darlene, was an adorable leopard shark.

"We bet the shark tank on this Christmas Extravaganza," Dash warned. "Gotta go."

He finished shaving around his silvery white goatee and combed back his prematurely gray hair. His blue eyes glinted from wrinkle-free eyelids, and his face was as smooth as a baby's posterior. But because of the color of his hair, he was often mistaken for an older man. That suited Dash just fine. The key to being a mystery shopper or tourist was to look the part.

"Today, I look like Samuel Finnegan, retired dentist." He tied a red silk cravat around his neck and grinned at his sparkling white teeth. "I'll be everywhere and nowhere. They all better be on their best behavior is all I have to say."

He couldn't help chuckling at his cleverness. If he was any lazier, he would call off the trip and let Gordon and his employees stew all week, wondering if he was among them. But then, he hadn't had a good feeling at the last progress report, and since he had no personal life, he might as well evaluate everything critically to optimize their chances for success. If all went well, he'd be back at Aunt Sharky's home for her New Year's Eve game night and celebrate a profitable end to a miserable year.

Chapter Three

The incoming blizzard blew ribbons of snow across Misty's windshield as she raced the old Jeep back the way she'd come. Now that the eastern hillside route was blocked off, she turned west toward the tiny community airport. It was slow going and even though she had four-wheel drive, her Jeep got stuck several times, forcing her to stop and dig the wheels out from the piling snow.

She was going to be late. Her only saving grace would be if the contractor was snowed in at the convention center with no place to go. She wondered if the cell towers were even working since her phone was mysteriously silent. Surely, Gordon would be breathing down her neck wondering where she was. Maybe he, too, got stuck in the incoming blizzard.

By the time she got close to the airport, the blizzard had fully arrived. Snow blew in circles around the Jeep. No one would be flying under these conditions. Sure enough, the lights on the runway were off, and no one manned the control tower. The runway had been recently plowed but was filling up with a thin layer of newly fallen snow. A snowplow had just finished plowing and was moving toward the side yard.

Misty zipped through the gate left open by the snowplow operator and zagged her Jeep onto the runway. Her tires kicking up a spray of snow, she floored the accelerator and swooshed through the fresh powder.

"Woohoo!" she whooped, going faster than it was safe. Her heart thrilled at how naughty she was, but hey, it was for a good cause. She, Misty Jolly, was the savior of Christmas Creek this year. The economy had been in a recession caused by rioting in the larger cities. All the marketing she did on social media was bringing flocks of fun-loving people to their safe haven town to celebrate Christmas. She would do her part to bring happiness to thousands of men and women, boys and girls, dogs and cats, and more.

The Jeep practically flew down the runway, and Misty could imagine herself driving a flying sleigh. Wouldn't it be magical if she pulled back on the steering wheel and her Jeep would sprout wings, accelerating higher and higher, going up, up, up through the flurries of swirling snow, soaring high up above the treetops.

Whhhooooosh!!! Roaaaar!!!! Thump, thump, thump, thump.

A huge shadow buzzed directly overhead, stopping Misty's heart cold. An airplane with its landing gear down dropped directly in front of her. Its tail bounced off her hood with a crunch. Misty slammed on the brakes. The Jeep skidding and swerving, she managed to avoid the airplane which was going much too fast.

It jumped over the end of the runway bumpers, careened through the chain-link fence, and crashed into a thicket of snowy bushes.

"Oh my! Oh my!" Misty screamed as she raced after the airplane. Someone could be hurt or dead. What if it was Mr. Weston?

* * *

Dash's body jerked in the harness as a flood of white slammed through the windshield of his Cessna turboprop. His face smashed into an onslaught of ice and snow, and his head rang with the clanging of jingle bells.

What the heck happened?

It took a moment for him to notice the utter stillness in his world of white. Where was he? And were his senses still operating? What if being blind meant seeing white and not black? Or being deaf because that whirring buzz in his ear took up all sound frequencies?

What if he were dead?

Dash groaned as pain crawled over his skin, then embedded deeper into his muscles and shook him to the bone.

Pain meant he was alive, right?

He tried opening his eyes, but all he saw was white. Was he going toward the light? Or was he already in a hospital bed?

Would he see his mommy? Surely, she'd make an exception, wouldn't she?

Would she tell him winter fairy tales full of snow goblins, frosty trollets, and ice sprites? Would she appear at his bedside with a plate of sky-blue frosted cookies sprinkled with coconut dots and sugar crystals, as light and sweet as a wintry sky? Could she forgive him for going for the green with his father and tolerating the many female marketing consultants his dad brought into the company?

"Mommy, forgive me," he whispered. "I may love money like Dad, but I'm staying far away from pretty women and definitely no marketing consultants or female mystery shoppers. If I die single and unattached, you'll know I never gave in to temptation."

But no, he couldn't die. Not yet. He was too young—not even thirty. He had to save Weston International from bankruptcy. He had to make his dad proud, and deep inside, there was something else he had to do, but for the life of him, or maybe the death of him, he couldn't recall.

Whatever it was, he had to get out of this world of white. His teeth chattering was a good thing. The pain and the numbing were good. He was thawing out and his nervous system was working.

Good.

His brain engaged. He was on his way to spy on Gordon Gills and the Christmas Extravaganza Experience at Christmas Creek. His big bet. His baby. His mark on the world.

Dash's muscles sprang into action. He brushed the snow from his face and unlatched the safety harness. He was inside the cockpit of his turboprop. The windshield was broken, and he'd crash-landed because some fool was driving a car on the runway.

He was late to a meeting with Gordon. Or was he meeting the event planner?

Dash's head whirled with bits and pieces. A scrap of conversation here. A wisp of a memory there.

"I'm in a rush. I have to go!" With a supreme effort, he pushed himself from the wreckage and crawled over the snowbank.

"Mister. Mister, are you all right?" A high-pitched female voice scratched the insides of his eardrums.

He pushed his hands over his ears and shook his head. Why was he so hypersensitive to sounds? His nose twitched and even with the snow blowing around him, he could smell her lilac fragrance and the nervous sweat blossoming from her body. It was a sweet, feminine, and sultry scent.

But he had no time to lose. He had to go, go, go.

"Mister. Let me help you." The same voice, now gentler and more dulcet, surrounded him as a pair of hands pulled on his arm. "Are you okay?"

She came into his vision. An angelic being with snow threaded through soft brown curls. Pink earmuffs and sky-blue eyes. Rosy cheeks and ruby-red lips. Had he died and gone to heaven?

His head shook and he said, "Wrrr. Wrrr. Wrrr." At least that was what it sounded like to his prickly ears.

"Oh my, we've got to get you to the hospital," the vision of beauty said. Her eyes were round with concern and an instant connection sparked. "I think my Jeep is still drivable. Are you by chance Mr. Weston?"

He was cold and his head shook harder. "Wrrr. Wrrr. Wrrr."

Why couldn't he speak? He was Dash Weston, wasn't he? Or was he trying on another persona? Which mystery shopper was he today? And where was he going?

Oh, right. Christmas Creek. Gordon Gills.

"Gggrrr. Grrr. Guuggg." The sounds from his throat didn't sound intelligible even to his sensitive ears.

"It's okay. I'll call for help." The woman who was surprisingly strong for her petite build slung his arm over her shoulder. She took a firm step forward, and he followed. Then another step, and he did likewise. His legs felt like heavy stumps, and his feet were numb. But somehow, they made it to her Jeep.

Was she the idiot who was driving on the runway?

"Rrrrr. Rrrrr. Ruuffff!" he accused her.

"It's okay. You'll be okay. You're in shock." She opened the door to her Jeep and shoved him into the passenger seat. "I'd call the sheriff if my phone worked, but I think the cell towers are down. Luckily, we have a new doctor in town. By the way, my name is Misty Jolly, and you're?"

She stared at him with expectant eyes and a warm smile—one he'd never seen directed to him.

Since his voice wasn't working and he didn't want to embarrass himself with more growls, grunts, sounding more like a coughing seal than a man, he wiggled his wallet from his pants pocket. He'd need to show the doctor his insurance card.

She rifled through his wallet and found his fake business card as well as a receipt. "Dr. Samuel Finnegan, it's nice to meet you. I see you have a reservation at the Christmas Inn at Southside Glen. You're in luck because I'm headed that way. But we're going to have to go back to town and report your crash to the sheriff. Oh, and you'll have to see Dr. Dale. I know you're in shock, but don't worry. I've got you."

He stared at her and had the strange impulse to wiggle his behind. What the heck was wrong with him? He hadn't hit his face that hard, had he?

Dash put his frozen fingertips, still encased in his leather driving gloves, to his face. His forehead was intact. Cheekbones, two of them. One chin with a cleft. Nose sharp and hawkish and deep ridged brows. Nope, he hadn't had a face transplant as far as he could tell, but what was wrong with his voice? Why couldn't he form words?

"Hey, you close your eyes and relax," the woman said. She truly was an angelic being. Her puffy pink jacket was the color of bubble gum, and those blue eyes of hers hearkened of clear wintry days skiing down the slopes and hot toddies in front of a fireplace.

He shook his confused head. Angels didn't drive Jeeps on runways and cause plane crashes. If he could speak, he'd call his lawyer and sue the down jacket off this blue-eyed miscreant. He fumbled in his pockets, but he knew already he wouldn't find his phone. It was in his briefcase, along with his laptop computer.

"You cold?" the concerned voice asked as she put the Jeep in gear and spun the tires. "Right. You can't talk. I'll put on the heat, Dr. Finnegan. You just close your eyes and rest easy. We'll get you to the doctor in no time at all. No time at all. No time at all."

Her voice seemed to fade into the recesses of his inner ear, and the white blankness returned to his vision, or maybe his eyes were closed or the blindness had returned. He faded to white, while her warm, sweet, comforting scent bathed his nose. Misty days and misty nights. Lost and found. Going far away and coming home. Sweet lilacs and a deeper scent, stirring a sense of longing and loss. What was he missing?

And then everything changed. He was still enveloped in whiteness, but he was running on his hands and knees. His breath steamed in his whiskers, and he was panting for air. He was in a hurry. He remembered. He had to get to Southside Glen. The project was a disaster and his dad was going to have his hide. He tore down the snow-covered trail and ducked underneath a split-rail fence to take a shortcut across a snowy meadow. The air was cold and crisp, and he practically flew down the hillside. A small pond was frozen solid. He was running so fast, he couldn't stop. His arms and legs splayed out and he slid across the icy pond on his belly. Scrambling up the slippery bank, he again used his hands and knees and was soon scurrying along a creekside, jumping fallen logs like he was a champion hurdler.

There was no time to marvel at his newfound athletic abilities or the fact that he was warm out in the elements, almost as if he was wearing a fur coat—although fur went out of fashion years ago. Nowadays, people freaked out at fur coats and regarded the wearer as a monster for wearing beaver hats or wolfskins, but nothing kept out the winter chill like a nice, thick pelt of fur.

Rushing, rushing, rushing, he raced down an unplowed road, wondering how he knew the way. His tongue hung from his mouth and saliva drooled. But he kept running, faster than humanly possible. He had to catch that event planner and her sneaky overcharging contractor in the act of cheating him, and he couldn't let on that he was Dash Weston until he'd gathered all the evidence and corrected their multitudes of mistakes.

Chapter Four

Worry furrowed Misty's brow as she turned the Jeep toward the town center. She was in deep doo-doo. The poor dentist she'd picked up was not only one of the tourists for the Christmas Extravaganza Experience but also injured because she'd been driving on the runway. Oh no! She was also responsible for the damage to his airplane, and from the wreck she saw poking from the snowbank, the entire front end was busted. Wasn't that where the propeller was on those planes? It wasn't just the money, which she didn't have, but the fact that she'd ruined Christmas for this poor old gentleman.

He'd been dazed and unable to speak. But despite his white hair and silver goatee, he had a stunningly strong face with piercing blue eyes behind owlish horn-rimmed glasses, a sharp nose, and a maniacal gleam like a treasure hunter struck by gold fever. His body was surprisingly muscular for his age, and his skin was tanned but not sun damaged like most old folks. No age spots. No wrinkles and nothing leathery. Just a firm tautness with the gleaming teeth found at the hands of plastic surgeons and cosmetic dentists. He was well dressed, as if he was on his way to a formal dinner. He wore a well-tailored gray wool suit, crisp white shirt with cufflinks, and a red silk cravat ascot around his neck. If she wasn't sure he was a dentist, she would have guessed he was one of the Christmas reenactment actors—one from central casting as a tap dancer or an extra in the black-and-white Bing Crosby Christmas movies. All he was missing was the top hat and walking stick, but he could have lost them in the crash.

Still, he was a curiosity, coming to a Christmas event by himself. Perhaps he was a grieving widower out to capture some of that Christmas spirit he so missed. Or he was an awkward bachelor, too tongue-tied to get a date, but nevertheless wanted to be included in holiday festivities. He seemed shy and reserved, but then again, most people couldn't get a word in when she was chattering to the trees.

No matter what, she, Misty Jolly, the nemesis responsible for his plane wreck, was obligated to show him as much Christmas spirit as she could muster. And hopefully, with fingers crossed, he would reciprocate with the spirit of forgiveness.

"We're almost to the health clinic," Misty said as she slid the Jeep through a covered bridge over the creek. "Too bad it's all the way back in town. Don't see why we have to have so many stoplights when we only have two main streets. You see, the main main street is called Main, and the other main street is really First Street, but since we never got a Second Street, we call it Only Street. The good doctor only moved here a year ago. Before then, if anyone got hurt, we'd have to drive clear over to Arcata to get to a hospital."

She glanced at the dentist who appeared to be dozing. Heavenly crickets. What if he wasn't asleep but dead? Or if not dead, he was in a coma.

"Dr. Finnegan. Are you okay?" She nudged him as she hung a fast turn on the corner of Main and Only Street. His body jerked with the turn and flopped back into the bucket seat like a dead fish.

The *whoop-whoop* of a cutoff police siren and the flashing red and blue lights in her rearview mirror halted her. Great. Just great. Another speeding ticket, and this time, aiding and abetting a possible dead body.

Again, she nudged the good dentist. He wasn't cold and stiff. That was a good sign, but was he breathing? It was hard to tell. He was so silent.

Sheriff Brad Wing lumbered toward her window with a ticket book flipped open. She knew the drill. A jawboning and warning to slow down, a strongly scrawled ticket detailing her transgressions, and then a hefty fine. Even though he was dating her older sister, Ivy, the sheriff was a stickler for rules and unbendable. No excuses and a real hard-ass.

"It's you again." He leaned down and sharpened his narrow eyes at her. "Misty Jolly."

"How do you know I'm not Merry?" she quipped, although she'd never get her sweet, quiet sister in trouble.

"Merry drives like an old lady. You? Like the red queen on steroids. This is the fifth ticket you've gotten this month, and you haven't paid for any of them."

"I don't have any money," Misty said. "Listen, I have a big job and if all goes well, I'll have enough to pay for all the tickets."

"I'm afraid the town cannot keep taking IOUs. I'm going to have to take you in and book you."

"Oh, you just can't," Misty protested. "I'm taking this poor man to see Dr. Dale. He's been in a plane crash. Can't you see? He looks dead, but I think he's not. I poked him, and he's not cold and stiff. No rigor mortis. Isn't that the technical term you police officers look for? So that means he's salvageable, and that means you, as a first responder, will have to escort me to Dr. Dale's clinic as fast as we can go. It's a matter of life and death."

The sheriff held his hand up to stop her from speaking. He ambled around the front of her Jeep and wiped his hand across the dented hood. Grimacing, he made his way to the passenger side and knocked on the window.

Dr. Finnegan didn't move, so Misty reached across him and lowered the window. "Can't you see he needs a doctor right away?"

"Mister. Are you okay?" Sheriff Wing shook the man's shoulder while glaring at Misty like she was putting on a show to get out of a ticket.

"Grrr. Grrrr. Roooaroh." A growling rumble issued from the silver-haired man's throat.

"Thank God, he's alive!" Misty squealed. "But it's still an emergency. He's been in a plane crash."

"Misty, the airport is closed and there are no flights coming in, so quit your jabbering," Brad grumbled. "I know you're putting on this giant Christmas Extravaganza full of minstrel shows and a gallery of Christmas movies, but you're on a public road being questioned by a peace officer, so no playacting."

Misty's jaw dropped to her knees. How could he accuse her of lying? Should she just forget about the wrecked airplane and her role in causing the crash? Maybe she should plead one of those amendments. No self-incrimination. She closed her mouth and zipped her lips. If he was so smart, he should be able to get Dr. Finnegan to speak.

The sheriff lasered in on said Dr. Finnegan. "Mister, could I have your name? Where are you from and what exactly are you doing in this speeding Jeep with Miss Jolly?"

"Ruh, ruhhh, ruff." The man clutched his throat. His eyes bulged as he stared at the sheriff. "Wwwoo, woof, wwoarh."

"I don't think he can talk," Misty said helpfully. "He's in shock. I told you he was in a plane crash and he barely escaped with his life. I found him in the wreckage and was bringing him to the doctor."

"Okay, then, let me take over." The sheriff opened the passenger door and helped the man out. He appeared limp, but let out a sharp yelp as if the sheriff had stepped on his foot. Was it her imagination or did the yelp sound like a dog's high-pitched cry of pain?

"Here's his wallet," Misty said. "He's a dentist, and he's staying at the Christmas Inn at Southside."

"Thanks. You may go now. Stop by the station later and I'll take your statement. No speeding." The sheriff took the man's wallet and looped his arm over his broad shoulder. Without looking back, he half dragged and half carried the man to the police cruiser.

Misty waited until they were safely on their way. She drove like a snail through the rest of the town, but as soon as she passed the town limit, she rocketed out of Christmas Creek like a cheetah after an ostrich. She was late. Late. Late!

Every minute and every second counted, especially with a contractor who nickeled and dimed every minute and every second, rolling up costs faster than the US Debt clock.

Misty pushed the Jeep to the limits. She raced up Bill Road, crossed Pill Road, and swerved down Fill Road. A flash of red flew across the road like a four-footed superman with a cape.

Misty floored the brake and caught a glimpse of the creature right before it disappeared underneath her Jeep. She gritted her teeth for the sickening crunch and peered hopefully in the rearview mirror in case the animal got away.

There was no sign of a red cape either in back of her or to either side.

Misty flung herself against the steering wheel, bracing herself as she tried to catch her breath. It was one thing to cause a plane crash, but at least the dentist walked away from it. But to kill a beautiful dog? Someone's beloved pet? What was she going to do?

A soft whine greeted her when she peered underneath the Jeep's undercarriage.

"Oh, sweetie. Are you okay? I didn't mean to run over you. Are you hurt?" Misty reached for the dog. It was shaggy with white-silver hair, and the red cape it wore looked like a man's silk cravat. Where had she seen one recently?

Misty shook off the déjà vu and petted the dog's head. "I'll take you to the vet. Dr. Kenes' practice is across from Dr. Dale's. Come on out. There's nothing to be afraid of."

The dog's nose twitched, and he made another pleading whine, but he crawled to Misty and licked her hand. She checked him for blood and finding none, she picked him up and placed him gently inside the Jeep.

* * *

Dash sat on the examination table while Dr. Colton Dale, a young fellow who looked more like a cowboy than a doctor, tapped his elbow and knees with a red rubber hammer. He wiped his eyes and blinked back the strange feeling of dashing through the snow. He was sitting in his underwear, wearing human skin, not fur, being examined by a medical doctor.

"Reflexes look good," the doctor said. "No sign of broken bones. Now, I'm going to touch your head for pain points. Can you let me know if anything hurts?"

Dash nodded. It was the least he could do.

The doctor felt various parts of his head, but truly, nothing hurt—not like the pain shooting all over his body on impact that had miraculously disappeared.

He shook his head and gestured to a pen and paper and made a writing motion with his hand.

"Got it." The doctor handed him the pen and paper.

Dash's hand shook as he stabbed at the paper with the pen. The pen wobbled in his fingers and wouldn't go the way he wanted. Instead of letters, all he could jot were scribbles and cross-outs. What was going on and why were his hands so clumsy? He must have neurological damage.

He threw the pen on the floor and flexed his fingers at the doctor. They were stiff and felt like claws.

"I'm going to place a call for a medivac helicopter to take you to the county hospital where they can do a scan," the doctor said.

Dash shook his head vehemently. His head wasn't aching and neither was any other part of his body. He was perfectly healthy other than not being able to speak. His tongue felt heavy and numb, and his fingers wouldn't cooperate with his brain, but nothing should stop him from his fact-finding mission on how Gordon Gills and the Christmas Extravaganza was coming along.

He pointed to his watch and then with both hands to the door, signifying he had to go.

"I can't in good conscience release you without knowing whether you have a bleed in the brain," the doctor argued.

Dash wasn't having any of this delay. He pulled on his pants and grabbed his shirt. Doctors could not hold a patient against their will. That much he knew.

He made gestures of writing a check and pointed to the clock to signify he'd do it later and then put on his shirt and tucked his cravat around his neck.

"Please don't walk out," the doctor pleaded. "You need to be under observation. You're welcome to stay until I can get the ambulance to come in here and fetch you."

Dash ignored the good doctor who appeared to be a brand-new one—quite young. He was quite used to using his older appearance to bowl over younger men. He grunted and put on his suit jacket, glaring at the doctor through his old-school glasses and shaking his jowls like a grumpy grandfather.

"Aye, I get you want to go, but do you have a friend who can pick you up?"

He nodded furiously, even though the only person he knew of was Gordon Gills, and Gordon didn't know what he looked like.

"In that case, Dr. Finnegan, can I have my nurse call your friend? I refuse to let you walk out of here alone."

He could refuse all he wanted, but Dash saw no way the deferential man could stop him. He put on his socks and shoes and pointed to the laces he was unable to tie.

The doctor bent over and tied them, still complaining. "You really shouldn't go out there alone. I'd like to see you the day after Christmas for a follow-up."

Fat chance. Dash shook his head dismissively. He straightened his cravat and checked his cufflinks. After refolding a red handkerchief in his breast pocket, he walked out of Dr. Dale's clinic without a backward glance.

Snow blew like a curtain around him, and the cold wind bit into his face. He stood in the middle of a whiteout and entered a white cocoon-shaped tunnel. He tied the silk ascot to his neck, tucked his head down, and braced himself against the stiff icy wind.

The sound turned off, and the world went black and white, like in the old movies. Wherever he was, he was in a rush, and just like in the dream, he knew where he was going. Stretching out his entire body, he ran between two parked cars and dashed across the—

Swish. Crunch. Judder, judder, judder.

A Jeep careened around the corner, ran over a snowbank, and sideswiped the two parked cars. It was coming right at him, and it was being driven by none other than the troublesome Misty Jolly.

Her eyes popped through the windshield, and his popped out in fright like in a cartoon. His heart caught in his throat, and he waved his arms, windmilling, ordering her to stop. Stop. Stop!

His hands flew over the hood of the dented Jeep, and the grill bumped his groin, lifting him off his feet. His belly slid over the hood, and he landed face-to-face with the she-demon, separated only by her frosty windshield.

The frosty fairy woman bounced out of the Jeep, and the doctor ran toward him from his office.

"Dr. Finnegan, are you okay?" Misty got to him first and dragged him off her hood. "I'm so sorry I ran into you."

Dash was sorely sorry too, but maybe he could bum a ride off her. Even better, he should steal her Jeep. Consider it a down payment toward the wrecked airplane she owed him.

He brushed by her and climbed into the driver's seat. The engine was still running, and he was sure he still knew how to drive.

"Whoa, whoa, where do you think you're going?" Dr. Dale grabbed the door to keep him from closing it. "You have a head injury. You're in no condition to drive."

"Wooaroahh, ruh, gggrrrr," he barked, and both Misty and the doctor stared at him as if he was acting weird.

He yanked at the door, but the misty maid managed to wedge her body against the frame, overwhelming him by her sweet scent and its sultry undertones, of early mornings in bed, tangled sheets, and steamy showers.

Something growled behind him and tugged the sleeve of his expensive suit.

Dash growled back, baring his teeth, and came nose to nose with a white wire-haired terrier just like the one he had as a boy. The dog barked in his face, and strangely, he understood him.

"Dash, long time no see," the dog said. "Remember me? I'm your guardian angel."

Chapter Five

Misty juggled her phone while navigating the multiple levels of the Southside Glen parking garage. She followed the arrows to park below the Christmas Village area where Dr. Finnegan had his reservations. "Gordon, listen, tell the contractor I'll be right there. Have to drop off a guest at Christmas Village and—"

"You're too late!" Gordon yelled over the phone. "Nasty Nate packed up and left. We're four days from opening the first Extravaganza Experience, and everything is unfinished. I'll call him and tell him you've finally arrived. I'm sure it'll be an extra mileage charge for him, not that he lives that far, but you know what a nickel and dimer he is."

"Then there's nothing I can do until he returns," Misty said. "Have you heard from Mr. Weston?"

"No, but his secretary said he left a while ago. I'm sure he'll be on the next flight once they open the airport."

"Great, then we have some time." Misty exhaled with relief. "Bye."

She turned to the dapper dentist who'd been taking deep breaths and trying to relax the entire drive. "We've arrived. You can open your eyes. See? Didn't I tell you I'd get you to your destination safely?"

The little terrier barked his approval and jumped on Dr. Finnegan's lap. He wagged his stubby tail as he smudged his cute little nose against the window.

"Oh, you little sweetie." Misty picked the terrier off Dr. Finnegan. "You're getting dog hairs on his suit. Now, you stay in the back while I help the dear dentist get settled in."

The dog barked and squirmed around, not at all looking like he'd stay put. Misty held him up to her, nose to nose, and made a funny face. "You're too cute. I bet you'd love to find a home for Christmas, won't you?"

The terrier licked her nose and panted his cute little doggie breath in her face.

"Oh, no. Not me! I'm way too busy to pay attention to a sweetheart like you." Misty gave him a pout. "But you're in luck. We're having a pet adoption event across from the petting zoo. I'll just bet you'll be one of the first ones auctioned off."

The tail wagging stopped, and the dog's face drooped.

"Now, don't you be looking at me all disappointed," Misty said. "Hey, maybe Dr. Finnegan would like to adopt you."

Since the dentist was still silent, Misty placed the terrier back on his lap. "He likes you."

The dog made little whirr, whirr, whirr sounds interspersed with sharp yaps and lower-pitched whines at the man who was as stiff as a mummy.

"If he's bothering you, I'll take him," Misty said with a sigh. "Let's get you checked in at the Village. It's one of our newest attractions. An entire indoor village to simulate a small town. I know you're booked at the Christmas Inn, but it's not quite ready. Our decorator went out of town to pick up supplies and is stranded by the blizzard. I think Mrs. Claus's Bed and Breakfast is open, and I'm sure she'll be able to accommodate you."

The dentist gave her a surly glare and grunted. He opened the door of the Jeep and stepped into the unfinished parking garage. He surveyed the construction materials with a disapproving eye and stomped toward the elevators as if he were on a mission.

"Wait. Dr. Finnegan. The electricity is out. We have to take the stairs."

He whirled around and marched toward the stairs, looking furious.

"Dr. Finnegan, please don't be upset," Misty pleaded. "The official Christmas Experience doesn't open for a few days, and we weren't expecting anyone. I don't know how you got the reservation through our website so early."

The dentist snarled at her. "Grrrr, grrr, rrrrr. Errrk."

"Dr. Finnegan."

"Grrr." He shook his head vehemently like a terrier shaking a rat.

"But Dr. Finnegan."

He snapped his teeth and growled while motioning her to shut up.

Misty chased after him. "Technically, the entire village is a construction site. I can't let you just barge in there. You might get hurt."

The dog trotted up to Misty and barked. She scooped him into her arms, glad for a friendly face.

"What is wrong with that man? I can't believe he's a dentist. They're usually nice and smiling all the time." She caught the grouch at the stairwell. "Dr. Finnegan, you really should calm down. At your age it isn't good to get all huffy and puffy. You might have a heart attack."

That stopped him cold. He glared at her with his maniacal blue eyes, then made a muscle with his bicep and hopped up and down, doing jumping jacks. Then as a display of dental prowess, he gritted his teeth and pulled both sides of his cheeks aside to show her his pearly whites.

"Okay, okay, so you've kept yourself in good condition for your age. But that still doesn't mean you can fly off on a rage or throw a temper tantrum just because you're disappointed."

He pointed at his face while making an astonished look and then swept his arm at the debris and construction trash sitting in the stairwell.

"Please, Dr. Finnegan, calm down. I know it's disappointing and you don't have your luggage. I'll make it up to you. I swear. Let's jus get you checked in with Mrs. Claus, and I'm sure you'll feel better jiffity-quick."

He again pointed to his mouth and he appeared to be speaking slowly, but it sounded like, "Grrr, woof, ruff."

The terrier repeated the same grrr, woof, ruff, but somehow, she got the message.

"Call me Sam?" she checked with Dr. Finnegan.

He crossed his arms and nodded, as if satisfied.

"Okay, I can do that," Misty said. "It sure saves a lot of syllables, five syllables versus one. I get it. If I had a name like Finnegan, I'd probably just want to be called Sam, too."

"Grrrrr," he warned.

"Sorry!" She kissed the terrier to give herself a distraction. "And what shall we call you?"

"Rrrf, wfff, woo." The little dog licked her and wagged his tail.

"I don't know what that translates to, but you're supposed to give me good luck. How about I call you Westie, so when Mr. Weston shows up, you can charm the pants off him and show him what a wonderful Christmas Extravaganza Experience I've produced here at the world-famous Christmas Village at Southside Glen."

Sam rolled his eyes and made a low, whining growl of disapproval, but Misty rolled her eyes back at him and gave Westie another kiss.

Was she imagining it?

Or was Westie giving *Sam* the look like he'd got one over him?

* * *

Mrs. Claus's Bed and Breakfast was no way and no how as ready as Misleading Misty made it seem. Dash felt like an unwelcome intruder while Mrs. Claus, who introduced herself as Constanza Zingerman, hustled and bustled around moving boxes, piling wreaths and garlands, and shoving potted miniature Christmas trees aside to clear a path. Boxes of decorations were in a disarray, and strips of festive wallpaper hung half undone.

The proprietress herself wrung her chubby hands and scrunched her brows with worry as she stared at the reservation form Misty showed her. "We're so delighted to have you, Dr. Finnegan. Luckily, I have one bedroom ready. It's the smallest one near the kitchen, but that means you're never far from food."

She trilled at the top of her lungs like she was an opera singer heaving her bosom at the finale.

He wanted to say he wasn't hungry, but his stomach chose that moment to make a loud, lurching roar.

"Oh my, sounds like we're wanting vittles," Mrs. Claus said.

The little rat terrier barked, wagging his stubby tail, and Misty smiled sweetly. "Con, do you think you can keep Westie for me while I meet Nate at Santa's Gazebo? I'm running late."

"I'll be glad to. Oh, you itty, bitty cutie." She enveloped the furball in her arms and squeezed him tight.

Dash's chest constricted, and he coughed from the sharp inhalation of the industrial-strength perfume overpowering his mysteriously enhanced sense of smell. He fought for breath, even though he wasn't the one having the life hugged out of him.

"Ruff, grrr, whelp." He grabbed Mrs. Claus's arms to keep Westie from suffocating.

"Whoa, are you flirting with me, Dr. Finnegan?" The heavyset woman shifted Westie to the crook of one arm while fanning her reddening face. "Or are you jealous?"

Dash shook his head helplessly. He was only saving the dog's life from being squeezed out of him. Instead, he held out his hands for the terrier.

"Oh, you do want him," Misty's voice lifted. "You two do look cute together."

Dash cuddled the puppy and shook his head. The dog was cute, but he was not. He was a man, after all, and he was sick of being talked down to. As soon as he got his voice back, he was going to set everyone straight. He was the VIP to be reckoned with. Oh, wait, he was supposed to be a mystery tourist, but still, a little or a lot of respect wasn't asking too much.

Unable to read his thoughts, Misty cocked her head and her eyes. "Don't they match?"

"They most certainly do," Constanza gushed. "Same silver-white hair. Ferrety look. Beady eyes down to the red cravat."

"Well then, I'll leave you two to get settled in," Misty said. "I have work to do. Busy. Busy. Busy."

Dash wanted to go with her, but Mrs. Claus took a firm grip on his arm and steered him like a jailer into the tiny room cramped wall to wall with rustic antique furniture.

"You are cranky, cranky," Mrs. Claus said. "Why don't I bring you warm milk and cookies and a doggy biscuit for the puppy? Then it's naptime for the two of you."

As soon as Mrs. Claus waddled toward the kitchen, Westie started his whirr, whirr, yip, whirr, talk.

"Great going, dude," Westie said. "How are you going to check up on Christmas Village when you're stuck here taking a nap? You should have been nicer to Misty and maybe she would have shown you around."

He growled and whined back, "Exactly how am I to order her around when I can't talk?"

"Play on her so she'd want to impress you," Westie said. "Get her to like you. Flirt a little. Make a move. Do I have to tell you everything? She was calling me sweetie, cutie, and all. I would have had her eating out of my hand if you hadn't been so cranky. Now we have to take naps."

"I'm not taking any nap. Now's our chance to escape."

"I kind of want a doggy biscuit."

"Then you stay in Mrs. Claus's lap. I'm outta here." Dash yanked open the door only to smash into Constanza's tray. Milk splattered over his face and hers, and cookies went flying.

"Whirrr, woof, ruff, whirr, grrr," Dash said, meaning to say, "Let me help you clean this up."

While Dash grabbed a hand towel, Westie gobbled up the dropped doggy biscuits and rushed out the door with a flash of his red cape like a superdog flying off on a mission.

Chapter Six

Dash's suit was ruined, soaked with warm milk and cookie crumbles, and Mrs. Claus didn't fare any better. Her fake fur trim was smeared with melted chocolate chips, and mascara ran down her face along milky trails.

"Oh, my, what a mess," she squealed as she dabbed Dash's suit jacket.

He meanwhile was sweeping the cookie pieces from the red-and-green-plaid carpet while having a weird loopy experience. While he was aware of the milk and cookie disaster, he was also trotting on four paws through a maze of construction materials, stepping over tinsel, dodging hay bales, and sniffing for Misty Jolly's delightful lilacky female scent.

"Are you okay?" Mrs. Claus asked. "Your suit needs to go to the dry cleaners."

He gasped, surprised at her closeness, and his nose was overwhelmed by her noxious perfume mixed with milk. Clamping his jaw tight because he didn't want to make any doggy sounds, he nodded resolutely while rueing that he'd lost Misty's trail. Hopefully, Westie was able to do better.

Grunting, Dash jerked away from Constanza's pawing hands when he realized she was undressing him.

"Waaah, waaarohhh," he said before remembering to shut up.

"What am I doing?" Constanza asked. "Wool and milk don't mix. Take off your suit right away, and I'll send it to the cleaners."

He didn't like her giving orders, but what she said made sense. What was he going to wear? He made a gesture, patting over his clothes and shrugging to indicate he had no change of clothes.

"No worries, we have plenty of costumes," Constanza said, trilling with operatic gusto. "After all, this is Christmas Village, and we provide costumes for all our guests. Here, let me take you to the dressing room."

At this point, he didn't care what he wore. He needed to catch up with Westie and Misty so he could see the project's lack of progress firsthand. His father was expecting a report, and if Christmas Creek failed them, they would have no choice but to close down stores and lay off employees.

Constanza combed through the costumes and picked out a red-and-white-striped sweater with a matching red-and-white-striped Santa's hat. "You can be Kris Kringle's little brother."

Dash didn't want to be anyone's little brother, but he was in a rush. He had to catch up with Misty before she destroyed evidence of Gordon Gills' mismanagement.

"Ah, the light-blue denim lederhosen will look great with the striped sweater, and oh look, a pair of red stockings to go with that red cape over your shoulders."

Dash shifted his weight from foot to foot, impatient to be on his way. He didn't care if he looked like a prison-striped yodeler. Rudely, he grabbed whatever clothes Mrs. Claus was offering and stomped back to his cubbyhole.

After pulling on the curly-toed sky-blue elf boots, Dash wrapped the red cape around his neck, waved goodbye to Mrs. Claus who was applying a green veggie goo moisturizer over her face, and dashed out the door.

"Have fun entertaining the kids," she hooted after him.

* * *

Misty took a can of spray paint used for construction marking and walked around the petting zoo area where she wanted the barn to be erected. She marked the various sizes for different animals: a pigpen, a chicken coop, a large bullpen for Larry the llama with signs to warn about spitting, and a general pen full of hay bales for the motley crew of goats and sheep.

"Where should I put the animals up for adoption?" She craned her neck and made a sight line from Santa's Gazebo to the petting zoo, visualizing the candy-cane trail and the sugar plum gallery, how it wound around nutcracker totem poles standing guard and exiting near the gift shop with the large screens to display the photos for instant printing and purchasing.

"Oh, I got it. I'll have the adoption area right after the gift shop, but wind the line beside it so the children can look at the pets while they're waiting for Santa and then ask Santa for the one they want. Brilliant! If I do say so myself." She held the spray can down and marked the dog area separate from the cat area.

"Woof, woof!" A happy bark shot out from behind one of the haystacks, and Westie romped up to her all bouncy and squirmy.

His little red cape flew behind him, and he really did look like a superdog.

"Oh, Westie. The adoption center's going to have the cutest doghouses painted like gingerbread houses. You're going to be one of the first ones adopted. I'm sure of it!"

"Grrrr, rrrr, whirr, yip." Westie bared his teeth and sneezed, not liking the idea at all.

"There you are!" Gordon shouted as he came around a pile of lumber trailed by the contractor, Nate Tallahan; his foreman, Jack; and his assistant, Dean, a scraggly teenage boy who wore hoodies year-round—winter, spring, summer, and fall. "We don't have much time. Show them the layout and get this thing done. Only a few days before the tourists arrive."

"On it." Misty pointed to the markings. "We'll get the children ready for Santa by funneling them through the petting zoo. This will relax them and also allow them to tire themselves out so they can stand in line without meltdowns. We'll mark the line with candy-cane light posts and have sugar plum fairies and toy soldier actors hang around to take pictures with the kids. Then, when they get close to Santa's throne, they will circle around the pet adoption area. Looking only, and no touching. We'll have plexiglass separating the Santa line from the pet enclosure, but as soon as the kids clear Santa's Gazebo, we can set the entrance to the pet area next to the photo gallery, perhaps even have a photographer in the pet area."

Westie squirmed in her arms, yipping and making growly, whirring noises.

"Sounds like he doesn't agree." The contractor frowned and rubbed his light-brown beard.

"Who cares what the dog thinks?" Gordon huffed. "Did you figure out a way to heat Santa's Gazebo without interference with the snow blowing machine?"

"The snow should not be in this area." Misty strode to another section of the village. "I'm thinking we put a mound of snow here and have plastic lids and laundry baskets to let the kids slide down. The snow blower could be placed above it, and it's close enough to the Christmas tree and ice rink to fit into the atmosphere."

"I still think Santa should be sitting in the North Pole." Gordon kicked a red-and-white-striped pole that was lying on the ground. "The snow should be swirling around him."

"The gazebo should be heated," Misty argued. "Having a shivering Santa won't do. My father won't sit on a freezing throne."

"Funny. Then why does he insist on the one at the town square?" Gordon challenged. "I'm pretty sure that one isn't climate controlled."

"Look. I'm still working on finding an appropriate Santa." Misty gritted her teeth. "My brothers won't do it because they think this gig is phony and fake. I don't see why you can't be Santa."

"How about you, Nate?" Gordon turned to the contractor. "You did a great job at the homeless shelter last year."

"And that's the only place I'll be Santa. Look, you have a town full of jolly old men. I'm sure given the right incentive, someone will do it if you pay them enough."

"Oh, look." The teenager tapped Nate. "Here comes someone. He looks like a cross between that elusive Waldo nerd and Kris Kringle."

Nate and Gordon whirled around and laughed at Dr. Finnegan, or *Sam*, who strode toward them in an aggressive manner. Jack and the kid had their mouths covered, but they, too were obviously amused at Sam's outlandish outfit.

Westie barked a greeting and Misty sputtered to stifle a giggle.

What the heck happened to Sam's Fred Astaire suit? The blue overall shorts over the red-and-white-striped sweater made him look like a cross between an American flag and a pig farmer on a poke. His white hair and goatee, along with the sharp nose and chiseled face gave him a Viking air, but as an emergency Santa, he'd do.

"Why Sam!" Misty sidled up to the dentist. "You're in time to help us with a few decisions."

"Is this the tourist you dropped off at Christmas Village?" Gordon's tone was belligerent. "Why didn't you tell him we weren't ready?"

"He had a valid reservation for the Christmas Inn," Misty said. "I saw the printout."

"That's impossible," Gordon said. "Tell your sister to fix the website. We can't have tourists running around this unfinished village."

Sam cleared his throat, but when he opened his mouth, nothing came out. He seemed to swallow his growls and barks, so Misty jumped to the rescue.

"This is Dr. Finnegan, a dentist. Didn't you say you have a sore tooth? In any case, he crashed his plane and lost his voice. We can't just turn him out of here, especially since he's exactly the type of customer we want." She put her arm around *Sam*. "Right, buddy? Looks like you love Christmas as much as me. No one dresses like Kris Kringle's little brother unless he lives and breathes Christmas. Trust me."

Sam's grimace deepened and he shook his head, probably embarrassed at being found out as a Christmas fanatic.

"Okay, you Nordic Santa you." Misty took *Sam* by the hand. "You're in time to help us position Santa's throne. Would you want it near the ice hill where the children are sledding or next to the pet adoption area?"

Sam hugged his arms and shivered, then shook his head. He took Westie from Misty and set him at the location where the gazebo was marked.

"See? Santa Sam says he wants to be near the pets and not the ice hill," Misty said. "We'd better do as he says."

Clap. Clap. Clap.

Gordon's beefy hands clapped slowly and somewhat sarcastically. "Is there anything else Santa wants? Misty, I'm sure you can accommodate."

"I, uh." It wasn't often that Misty had no words. What exactly was Gordon implying?

Sam did his throat clearing again, as if he wanted to run interference for her, but of course, no words came out. Westie trailed Gordon's ankles and barked ferociously, yipping and yapping to defend her honor.

"What's this dog doing here?" Gordon demanded. "We have a lot of work to do before Mr. Weston shows up. Take him to the pound before he messes up the decorations."

Misty picked up Westie and held him protectively in the crook of her arm. "This dog belongs to Dr. Finnegan, our esteemed guest, as in *paying* customer!"

"I don't think we allow pets in our properties," Gordon said. "In fact, Mr. Weston was very specific that all animals be kept at the petting zoo and not allowed anywhere close to the lodgings."

"Well, Mr. Weston isn't here, and I'm sure Sam and Westie will be gone before the airport reopens." Misty was taking liberty to speak for the poor dentist. "In fact, let me see about putting him up at the Christmas Cottages in town. Then maybe he'll get a real Christmas Creek experience without worrying about a pet policy."

"Excuse me, Misty, but your bread is buttered here at Southside Glen," Gordon countered. "You have no time to be gallivanting around town putting people up at other venues. This is the premiere Christmas destination of the known universe, deserving your full attention."

"I fully understand, but if Santa here wants his dog, then Santa gets to have his dog. Think of Westie as the Christmas Village mascot."

Gordon's eyes bulged like they were going to pop. "Whatever you do, there better not be any screwups when Mr. Weston arrives."

The workmen's faces ping-ponged back and forth, watching their altercation, but *Sam* made a timeout sign with his hands and shook his head, frowning. He then pointed to the lumber and made hammering motions.

"Right, you all need to get to work," Gordon said. "Time's a-wasting, and I'm not paying for spectating. Now that Misty marked the areas, get everything put up and ready. Holly and Ivy will be here tomorrow to decorate, so all the walls and facades need to be up, including the replica of the Gills Mansion."

After Nate and his workmen ambled off to work on the gazebo, Gordon put on a salesman's smile and extended his hand to *Sam*. "Dr. Finnegan, welcome to Christmas Village at Southside Glen. Please accept my apologies for the disarray. Our attractions aren't open for several days, and I'll be glad to refund your money."

Sam shook his hand, but waved dismissively with his other hand. Then he turned around in a giant circle with his arms spread out as if visualizing the grandeur of the finished indoor Christmas setting. He made sweeping motions at the area where Misty suggested the ice hill, then gawked at the tall artificial tree and studied the detail on the gingerbread house.

"Gordon, I don't think Sam wants a refund," Misty interjected. "I'm betting he's having the time of his life being in on the behind-the-scenes preparations for the grandest Christmas Extravaganza Experience ever!"

"In that case, let's get to work," Gordon said. "All the construction has to be done by end of the day. Misty, I don't care how late these guys have to stay. They need to finish before you let them leave."

"It's going to cost overtime," Misty warned, and she thought she heard *Sam* growl, or was it Westie?

"Mr. Weston isn't going to like it," Gordon warned. "Think outside the box. Who else can help?"

"I'll call my brothers," Misty said and then brightened. "Sam, can you hold a nail gun?"

Sam nodded eagerly, giving her the okay sign.

"Then you're drafted." Misty hooked his arm with hers. "We'll give you a refund anyway, but I'm warning you. You're going to earn every penny of it."

"Woof, woof, woof!" Westie barked happily, and Misty thought she heard a voice say, *Sam would love to be the Santa if you can't find one.*

Misty gave *Sam* a thumbs-up. "Thanks! You're a lifesaver."

Chapter Seven

Misty had to hand it to *Sam*. Even though he was a dentist, he rolled up his sleeves and hammered and nailed. He was a pro with the circular saw, and he worked late into the evening, despite Constanza coming by to feed him sandwiches and other treats "on the house."

She woke early the next morning and drove to Southside Glen shortly before sunrise. The traffic was sparse, and she didn't almost run over anyone—not even a deer.

Her first stop was Mrs. Claus's Bed and Breakfast.

"Yip, yip, yap!" Westie greeted her at the doorway with his stubby tail twitching. She sensed a thought bubble over him saying, *Sam thinks you're awesome,* but shook it off. She was more exhausted than she was aware of.

The scent of bacon and eggs, along with the bubbling of a coffee percolator drew her into the kitchen.

"Your visitor is being well taken care of," Constanza said. "Poor boy had to soak in the tub after all that hard work yesterday."

Misty reached into her purse for her checkbook. "Let me cover his meals. We can't charge these extras to the construction budget. Mr. Weston will have a cow."

"I don't see why not," Constanza said. "Sam worked as hard as any of the workmen, and he's not even charging for his labor. He was all smiles, despite being exhausted, and I do believe he's enjoying himself to the fullest."

"Take the money," Misty urged. "Just don't cash the check until after Christmas. I should have some cash coming in if all goes well."

Someone cleared his throat, and both Misty and Constanza spun around to find *Sam* standing at the doorway. He gave Misty an obvious once-over that made her face heat, and she wondered how much of the conversation he'd heard.

"Good morning, Sam, dear," Constanza said. "Ready for another hard day's work?"

She herded *Sam* to the breakfast table and hovered over him, serving him eggs, bacon, pancakes, and coffee.

"I'm off to supervise," Misty said. "And thanks, Sam, for helping out. Don't feel obligated."

Westie whined, and another thought came over her. *Don't worry, it's a pleasure for Sam to serve.*

The way he looked at her, like *she* was good enough to eat, made her heart flutter in a good way, but she had no time for flirting, especially with all the work that remained and the threat of Mr. Weston showing up unannounced at any moment.

"You must stay for breakfast," Constanza said. "On the house."

"I've already ate," Misty said. "Just don't let Mr. Weston hear how much food you've been giving away to the workers."

She noticed *Sam* studying the syrup patterns on his pancakes while Westie looked up from crunching on the bacon, as if he understood them.

Dismissing it as nerves, she pasted on a smile and bade them goodbye.

Gordon was at the gazebo, pacing around with a clipboard. "About time you arrived. How much do we owe that dentist for all the work he did? I hope he's not charging dental rates."

"I do believe he's having a ball," Misty said.

"Then you're going to have to keep him happy so he'll keep having a ball," Gordon said. "We can't afford more cost overruns."

"I know. At least my sisters and brothers aren't charging. Dad already announced our project at the tree lighting event last week."

"What got him to support us?" Gordon asked. "I thought he was against us competing with the town square businesses."

"He loves us, and he loves this town," Misty said. "You ought to know he might have his opinions, but family and community always come first. If we're successful, the town's successful."

"Misty, we're here!" Holly's voice chirped from behind a dumpster piled high with construction debris. "Come help me unload the van."

"There you are, honey," Gordon said in a puffed-out heroic voice. "How'd you get through the blizzard?"

"Told you my van's a flying sleigh," Holly replied, kissing him with a loud smack. "Holly's Jolly Elves to the rescue. Got Ivy with me and a police escort from Brad."

A gaggle of giggling high school girls emerged from Holly's van. She'd driven through the service entrance and parked next to the dumpster in the backlot area.

Ivy's decorator van pulled up alongside Holly's. While Holly's van was out and loud, painted with bright-red holly berries and the blazing words, "Holly's Jolly Elves," Ivy's was calming and sedate with curlicues of ivy surrounding the words, "Ivy's Sweet Sets," in an old-fashioned script font.

More women tumbled out of Ivy's van which was dragging a trailer full of facades and canopies to create background scenery. Among them was a grouchy gray tomcat, Figgy, who belonged to her brother's girlfriend, Kitty.

"I'm so glad you're all here!" Misty jumped up and down. "Ivy, I need you to set up the Gills Mansion sets. It's on the other side of the mock town square where the tree stands. Did you bring real ivy to trail over the gates? Everything has to look real and not made-up like a theme park."

"Even though the real Christmas Creek is right out there," Ivy said. "I mean, why are you guys doing a replication of Christmas Creek when people can just go to the real one?"

"Because of things like blizzards, icy rain, and freezing temperatures." Misty pointed to where Nate and his crew were constructing Santa's throne. "It's heated. You know how Dad's always complaining about his old bones and how the cold gets to him after hours of sitting outdoors?"

"He's a jolly old elf," Holly said. "He enjoys sitting outside with the fresh air and the occasional snow flurry."

"Yes, but in here, everything's within a few hundred yards. You can sit on Santa's lap, adopt a pet, get your picture taken with Christmas characters, drop off a toy at the toy drive, stop by for a hot toddy, play elf poker, and then go ice-skating at the rink without having to drive all over the county on icy roads and braving the elements."

"Well, Dad can't be two places at the same time. You'll need another Santa willing to sit on the heated throne," Holly pointed out. "And no, Gordon's not doing it. He's going to preside at all three of the fake Gala Balls as the Winter Prince."

"Dad might do it if you come to all of our pre-Christmas activities," Ivy repeated her parents' continual request for her presence at the traditional events.

"I can't! I'm running the show here." Misty put her fingernail to her teeth before jerking her hand back. She'd already chewed off the tip of two fingernails. "Besides, I might have found a ready and willing Santa. He's quite a bit younger than Dad, and not plump at all, but these days, people appreciate a muscleman Santa, I think."

Sam had evidently gulped down his breakfast, because he was fast approaching Holly's van, looking for something to do.

"Who?" Her sisters and their entourage swiveled their heads, looking for a likely candidate.

"That handyman contractor?" Holly asked. "I thought he's the homeless shelter Santa."

"No, psst, over there." Misty pointed to *Sam* who took it upon himself to remove cartons of ornaments from Holly's van and place them in front of the gigantic artificial tree underneath the convention center's dome.

"That's your Santa?" Ivy's jaw dropped. "He looks an Alpine ski instructor. Wow!"

"You're not supposed to be looking." Holly bumped Ivy's hip. "Your cop's got a giant nightstick."

The two older twins giggled, and Misty felt her mouth water at the thought of skiing down a snow-covered valley with *Dr. Sam*. She'd bet he was athletic from looking at his build. No matter what, it was obvious from his eagerness to decorate the tree that he loved Christmas as much as her family.

"Misty? I know that look." Holly nudged her. "Why don't you introduce us to that hunky Waldo Claus? He's even got the round glasses."

"He might be dressed like Waldo, but he's no nerd," Misty said. "He's tanned and sharp like a buccaneer pillaging the Spanish Main."

"Oh, and look at that dog!" Ivy squealed as Westie chased Figgy around the tree. The tomcat hissed and spat, clawing at the silly puppy while Misty scrabbled to rescue him.

He rewarded her with copious licks on her face, but *Sam* paid them no attention. He was intently laying out the ornaments into a pattern while interweaving them with strings of colorful lights.

"Dr. Finnegan, er, Sam," Misty said. "You don't have to do any of that. The decorators are here."

"Hi, I'm Holly Jolly, and these are my elves." Holly pirouetted around in her red holly berry outfit, complete with dangling holly berries across her bosom. "We're the official decorators of Christmas Village."

"And I'm Ivy Jolly, owner of Ivy's Sweet Sets. I'm aiming to create all of Christmas Village's backdrops as well as the nightly northern lights show." Ivy made a flourish with a green wand toward the hanging reflexive sheets strung across the ceiling.

"Sam, would you like to supervise?" Misty sensed *Sam* was determined to help. "Since you volunteered to be the village Santa, we'd like you to not just *like* your surroundings but to *love* them."

Sam's blue eyes glinted as he surveyed the incomplete village. He nodded curtly and clapped his hands, then made gestures to each of Misty's sisters.

"Sam can't talk because he's in shock after his plane crash," Misty said. "But he has a way of making his wishes known, don't you?"

She gave him a wink, and the gleam in his eye sent a shiver of delight over her skin. He didn't look at day over thirty, other than his silver hair, and now she wondered if he was playing a Christmas character to such an authentic degree that he'd dyed his hair.

Suddenly self-conscious, Misty averted her gaze and straightened *Sam's* bright-red cravat. "To thank you for helping, would you like to come to my parents' house for dinner?"

He returned her a curt nod, then made rolling gestures for everyone to get to work. Taking Westie, he marched from station to station, attraction to attraction, setting to setting, overseeing the design of his village while Westie barked encouragement.

"Stop staring." Holly nudged Misty. "Your eyes are burning a hole in those overall shorts of his. I do say. He's got nice legs underneath the lederhosen. Why don't you ask him to the Gala Ball?"

"Which one?" Misty sputtered, realizing there were three fake ones at Southside and a real one at the Gills Mansion Christmas Eve.

"Why, all of them. I'm sure Kris Kringle's brother Sam Single has the energy and endurance to keep up with you. Why, look at him go."

Look indeed. Misty's pulse rate quickened at how fast *Sam* dashed around the unfinished Christmas Village.

"I can keep up with him," she declared and power walked after him.

* * *

Dash hated to admit it, but Misty and her sisters were one heckaluva team of elves. They were all easy on the eyes, glittery and glamorous, and their light-hearted chatter to the background of Christmas jingles made quick work of a million tedious tasks.

Like a hive of busy and cheerful bees, the team painted the gazebo with candy cane stripes, strung up twinkle lights—red, green, and white—wound garlands around every picket fence, and nailed wreathes to all the storefront doors.

Dash caught himself several times whistling to "Jingle Bells" or "Deck the Halls" and he had to stop himself from wiggling his butt to "Santa Bring My Baby Back to Me." But he couldn't stop his wandering eyes from following Magical Misty around.

The woman had batteries that never ran dry. She was everywhere, directing the contractors, unrolling wrapping paper, holding up ladders, spraying fake snow and frost on windows, and dancing merrily between each station.

As for Westie, he and the cat named Figgy fought and spat, growled and tumbled, dashing underneath trees and jumping over hay bales. They streaked through a pile of tinsel and dragged glitter and tinsel threads all over the village.

"Boo!" Misty covered his eyes from the back. "How are you enjoying your stay?"

He took hold of her thin hands and held them, turning his head to look back at her. He wanted to say it wasn't what he expected, but of course, he'd been through a shock and lost his speech capabilities.

So he did the only thing he could do. Nod and turn himself around so he stared into those misty-blue eyes of hers.

"It's coming together, isn't it?" she said softly. "We still have to get the ice-grooming machines fixed, and I'll need fresh bales of hay. Oh, and what do you think about a horse-drawn carriage to drop off visitors at the Christmas Inn?"

He scrunched his nose and shook his head, making a circle with his hand to signify horse dung.

"Yikes, you're right. Wouldn't want to have to clean up after them," she said. "Guess that's why my parents insist that outdoors is best. They're having a Christmas caroling marathon after dinner. It starts underneath our town Christmas tree. Do you want to come with me?"

He grinned at the thought of having dinner with Misty with the added bonus of checking out the town square's famous Christmas tree. He'd heard it was planted in the ground and was decorated to the hilt, including a brand-new star every year—sort of like the Times Square New Year's ball.

"I'll take it as a yes," Misty said, tilting her face up to him. She was close enough he had the insane urge to kiss her, but of course, that wouldn't do. He was on an important mission, and he couldn't allow random emotions to derail him from making sure Christmas Village was profitable.

"Oh, and you can wear this to dinner. No worries," Misty said.

He smiled and nodded, hating his inability to speak. This wasn't like him to be so passive.

"Think we can call it a day?" She took his hand and led him around the central square where the gazebo had been set up and painted. "Look at the progress we made."

He wanted to say they had only a few more days before opening, and that the trash needed to be removed, the sets still had gaps, and some of the building facades were not anchored in place. The food court needed fake snow and the convention center ballroom did not yet resemble the insides of the Gills Mansion, but dang it, his tongue was tied.

"I really want to thank you, Sam Finnegan." She squeezed his hand. "Let's pick up Westie so I can show you the real Christmas Creek."

"Whirr, whoo, woof." He meant to correct her that the convention center was every bit as real as the old part of town, but she only chuckled.

"Don't worry. Westie can translate. Sometimes, when he barks, I hear voices. You won't call me crazy and have me committed, will you?"

Oh no. He wouldn't have her committed to anything other than finishing the Christmas Village project. He could practically count the profits already. If the next few days went as well as today, he could give his father a glowing report and maybe next year, they'd invest in a few more Christmas Villages in small towns across the USA. And he could hire Misty Jolly to lead the project.

"You have that weird glow in your eyes again." Misty had a dreamy look in hers. "What are you thinking about?"

Projects, profits, and you, he thought, but instead of speaking, his lips pressed themselves softly against hers. Since she was as enticing as a stocking stuffed with cash and she kissed him back, he allowed himself the pleasure of plunder.

True, he still hated the Christmas song and dance, but for profits' sake, he could keep up the act until December 26, especially with Misty Miracle in his arms.

Chapter Eight

Ordinarily, Dash would have asked a woman if she wanted a kiss, not simply taken one. He wasn't raised to be a cad—especially not by a mother who had to endure his father's multiple mystery shopping partners.

He backed off slightly, stroking the curls that framed Misty's face like a soft cloud, only to have her snuggle closer, clearly enjoying the kiss. Good. He wasn't out of bounds, and besides, even if she complained later on, she couldn't connect him to Weston International.

He hugged her tighter, wondering if there was a middle ground between his father's womanizing and his Aunt Sharky's watchful eye. All work and no play made an effective executive. He couldn't tell anyone the number of tight jams he'd gotten the company out of due to his investigative skills while not getting distracted by a pretty skirt.

Not that Misty was a distraction. No, not so. She was a direct target of his inquiries. She and Gordon had better watch out because he wasn't going to reimburse them for their mismanagement. He'd overheard the contractor jack up the rates for a supposed "rush" job. If it were up to Dash, he would have fired the contractor already. He didn't pay for shoddy work, and the entire indoor snow thing was ripe for disaster. Hadn't they already paid to have the water main break cleaned up? And why should they be responsible for fixing the broken ice-grooming machine?

"You okay?" Misty whispered, breaking off the kiss. "I'm not overwhelming you, am I? I'm usually not this naughty, but as you seem tongue-tied, I guess, well, sorry."

He gave her a reassuring nod and smiled. Then he tapped the tip of her nose endearingly. She really was pretty and so much alive. Full of energy and enthusiasm. He almost had a case of whiplash from whipping his neck around, watching her prance from one side of the village to the other like one of the fast-moving characters in an old silent movie.

"Ahem." The deep voice of Gordon Gills hovered over them. "Dr. Finnegan, if you'll excuse us, I need a word with Misty."

Dash backed off and melted into the woodwork.

Since Misty had invited him to her home, he'd better check with Mrs. Claus about his suit. It wouldn't do to wear this goofy Kris Kringle's little brother outfit outside of Christmas Village. What if his picture appeared in one of the promotional brochures? Aunt Sharky would never let him hear the end of it. Even his mother would be amused, knowing he'd never catch a girl looking like a Christmas Waldo lurking in a crowd of fake Santas.

He was walking toward Mrs. Claus's Bed and Breakfast when Gordon's angry voice turned his head.

"What the hell do you think you're doing playing tongue hockey with the visitor?" Gordon scolded Misty as if she were his younger sister. "Were you watching over Nate when he turned on the snow machine? He claims the temperature is too high to get the snow to form, much less stick, and he recommends we turn off the heater near Santa's Gazebo."

Dash could have told Gordon that low temperatures were needed to make snow. The entire idea of an indoor Christmas Village was to have comfortable temperatures and climate control. If a visitor wanted snow, there was plenty of it outdoors. The type of person who could come to an indoor Christmas Experience was the same type who visited theme parks or the Las Vegas Strip as opposed to roughing it in real on-the-spot locations. They wanted everything prepackaged, hygienic, safe, and contained.

"We already advertised balmy temperatures for Christmas Village," Misty argued. "The website shows Santa wearing a Hawaiian shirt and board shorts. I thought we agreed to put the ice hill on the other side of the village. We can blow the snow there."

"You have no idea what Nate's crew is charging to move all of that snow indoors with no guarantee it won't melt." Gordon shook papers at Misty. "This is way over budget. It's as hot in here as Miami in the summer."

"We turned up the heat so the decorators would be comfortable," Misty said. "You were the one who said most of our visitors were coming from Southern California and wouldn't know how to dress warmly."

Gordon threw up his hands. "You're the event planner. You should have known we couldn't have ice-skating, sledding, and blowing snow while letting visitors walk around in shorts."

A deep growl rumbled from Dash's chest, and he rushed back to Misty's side, inserting himself to shield Misty from Gordon's tirade. A barrage of growls and vicious barks snarled from his throat. Westie dashed underneath his legs and grabbed Gordon's pant legs, growling and making whirring sounds in his little throat.

"Sam. It's okay," Misty said. "Gordon and I were just having a discussion."

He wanted to argue. Wished he had words. But all he could do was growl deeper and more threatening.

"Listen, Dr. Finnegan." Gordon shot him a weirdo-alert glance. "I offered you a refund, and I'll be glad to rebook you once our Christmas Extravaganza Experience is up and running. Now, if you'll kindly excuse us, I'm dealing with my employee here."

Dash clamped his arm around Misty's shoulder and stuck to her side. This project was his, and they were both working on his behalf.

"Please, excuse us." Gordon enunciated the words more strongly.

Dash shook his head. He pointed at himself and tried convey his right to be present.

"Sam?" Misty squirmed in his arms. "Can you be a dear and meet me at Mrs. Claus's in twenty minutes? You're really sweet to come to my defense, but Gordon is practically my brother-in-law, and this discussion is about business. Nothing personal."

Nothing personal, my foot, Dash thought. He gave Gordon a steely-eyed warning that turned into a staring contest while Westie made growling noises at Gordon's ankles.

Those growling noises were intelligible, at least to Dash. "Leave me with Misty, and I'll let you know what they talked about."

Gordon broke eye contact to shake off the dog, so Dash counted it as a win.

He gave a loud huff that sounded like a Great Dane's sneeze and watched as Misty picked the terrier up and tucked him in the crook of her arm. No doubt she was perfectly capable of handling Gordon and didn't need his protection, but no way was Dash going to stand back and let Misty take the blame for the snafu. The weather outside was frightful, and that was exactly why they designed the climate-controlled Christmas Extravaganza Experience. Misty was right to push back on the indoor snow.

He was paying good money for Gordon and Misty to figure out the best mix of events and activities for his guests, but he couldn't break his cover just yet. Not until he'd gotten the scoop on Christmas Creek's founding family, the legendary Jollys. It would make business sense to understand his main competitors in this small neck of the woods, and Misty Jolly was the right person to give him inside information.

* * *

Misty was itching to get to Mrs. Claus's so she could pick up *Sam* and take him home. Ever since her older two sisters got longtime boyfriends, her parents have been acting like she and Merry were destined to be nuns. Well, truth be told, she was way too busy to date, and while Merry wasn't much of a dater, she'd been hanging around a young widower and his daughter, ostensibly for babysitting purposes.

It was hard to stand out in a family of seven children: three boys and two sets of girl twins. While Holly and Ivy got all the Christmassy attention, she and Merry were usually side characters in their family Christmas plays. They got leftover costumes as fairies, angels, dolls, and candy canes, while Holly was known as Santa's chief elf and Ivy was the reigning winter princess.

Merry didn't mind staying in the background, but Misty could never sit still and she needed constant stimulation and praise. It wasn't easy deciding what she wanted to do in life. Everything she tried was already done by one of her older siblings. The only way she could get any attention was to run faster and do more, and that was why she signed on to Gordon's Triple Christmas Extravaganza deal.

The Ultimate Christmas Experience would be concentrated in a fantasy Christmas Village contained in the Southside Glen convention area. Visitors would be saturated with everything Christmas—one activity after another, getting the opportunity to try it all without any breaks or downtime. Everywhere they turned, another authentic Christmas adventure would stare them in the face. There would be the traditional Santa's throne, obviously, but also an international foods and crafts bazaar showcasing Christmas around the world and how people celebrated in all climates. Gift buying opportunities abounded from jewelry to toys and trinkets. One of the highlights would be the northern lights show underneath the dome where the giant Christmas tree stood. Everything would be perfect if they could have snow.

Which was why she and Gordon were peering over the spreadsheets and unable to agree to a plan.

"It wouldn't feel like Alaska to have northern lights without snow," Misty mused. "But at the same time, we have a tropical Christmas in Hawaii spread in front of the model cruise ship and we can't have the hula dancers freezing their grass skirts off."

"I agree, but these costs will eat up any profit." Gordon gritted his teeth. "I don't see Mr. Weston approving the refrigerated boxcar that would pre-freeze the snow before blowing it out into the courtyard. How the heck will we keep it from melting?"

"I've an idea. We're in the middle of a blizzard. We can bring the snow in from outside. I'm sure there are tons of it piling up."

"The contractor will charge an arm and a leg to move the snow." Gordon shook a written estimate. "This is way over budget."

"Then maybe we can open the dome and let the snow fall down into the atrium. We'll have fans that direct the snow to the North Pole and away from the hula dancers."

"That is the stupidest idea ever. Santa's Gazebo is right underneath the northern light show. Now you're going to let in the cold air and freeze Santa's tush on his throne."

"Well then, you're the boss," Misty said. "You tell Mr. Weston the bad news. I'm off to family dinner."

"Are you going to be able to get your dad to be Santa? Now that we've made the throne padded and heated?"

"I thought Sam volunteered."

Gordon pointed his finger at her so close to her face she had to take a giant step back. "No, you volunteered him. The poor man can't even talk. We can't have a barking Santa body builder who looks younger than Mrs. Claus by a mile. I'm betting he dyed his hair white just to trick women like you into thinking he's a distinguished dentist."

"Well, I saw his driver's license and his business card, and it says he's a dentist practicing in San Francisco."

"Doesn't mean you ask him to our family dinner," Gordon groused. "I wasn't invited until I became Holly's boyfriend officially."

"Too bad for you, Gordon Gills, but whether Sam's an official boyfriend or a tongue-hockey partner, he's my guest. Mom and Dad have been pestering me on why I don't have a boyfriend, and since Sam conveniently crashed his plane at our airport, I owe it to him to show him around."

"I'm surprised Brad hasn't arrested you for driving on the runway," Gordon said. "You're way too reckless. Anyway, I'm going to be late to dinner. I have to run these numbers and give Mr. Weston a choice. If he wants to spend on the refrigerated unit, we can have snow brought in daily."

"I'm glad you're the boss and not me," Misty added a singsong whistle. "Come on, Westie, let's go see if Sam Single's ready to go."

Chapter Nine

"My, my, Dr. Finnegan, you're looking spiffy," Mrs. Claus said to Dash as she put a top hat over his head and handed him a walking stick.

"Thanks for getting my suit dry-cleaned so fast. How'd you get it to the cleaners through this blizzard?"

The matronly woman wiggled her hips and winked. "Mrs. Claus always gets her wish."

He twirled the walking stick. "Well, I do sincerely thank you. Misty is meeting me here to take me to dinner at her parents' place."

"Then it's a good thing you got your voice back. It must have been awful the shock you went through."

No kidding. He had yet to check out the damage to his turboprop, or even file an insurance claim. Speaking with growls and barks wouldn't have worked on the phone, and he hadn't even checked in with his secretary—or given a report to his dad.

"Woof, woof, whirr, ruff, rrooo." Westie scampered up the path toward the bed and breakfast and slipped over the threshold. "Woooah, whoo, worrk, woof, wrrr."

Dash understood the barks to say, "You won't believe what they're saying about you. Gordon doesn't think you look the Santa type, and Misty likes playing tongue hockey with you."

"My, my, you're yappy today." Mrs. Claus picked up the terrier. "You sure have a lot of tales to tell."

"You understand him?" Dash asked. He almost added the word, "too," before swallowing it back. He got his voice back. Did it mean he was cured of the shock? He glanced in the mirror over the rustic hewn entrance table. If his hair weren't already white, he would have said the shock did it to him. Maybe he ought to dye it dark brown and look his age. Misty looked to be in her early twenties, and he didn't want to look like her father.

"No, I don't speak dog," Mrs. Claus replied. "But it sure looks like he's telling you a story."

"Westie! Wait up." Misty's voice came toward them through the half-open front door. "Sam might not be ready."

Dash didn't want his cover blown, and if they knew he could speak, Misty's parents would ask him a million questions, like how old he was, when he got his "dental" degree, and would soon figure out who he really was.

"Do me a favor," he whispered to Mrs. Claus. "Don't tell anyone I can talk. Especially Misty. She's only taking me to dinner with her family because she feels sorry for causing my plane crash and the shock she put me through."

"Oh, I'm sure there's more to that than pity." Mrs. Claus winked. "But my lips are sealed. You go on now and milk it for all you can."

She chortled as Westie lifted his head and made his whirring growly and yipping noises that said, "Better sneak scraps under the table for me or I'll spill the beans."

Misty appeared at the threshold of Mrs. Claus's cottage, slightly out of breath and looking as radiant as a winter fairy. Dash couldn't get over how lucky he was that she was the project coordinator. As far as he could tell, she was doing the best job she could, but Gordon was blaming her for his mistakes. He'd have to set this straight once he could get to his email to remind Gordon that all cost overruns would come out of Gordon's share of the profits. It was only fair. Gordon got a performance bonus in proportion to the profits in exchange for Weston International owning all trademarks and the rights to replicate or improve on the Christmas Village concept worldwide.

Misty streamed through the open doorway and straightened Sam's cravat. "You look, like wow! The top hat, hey is that mistletoe hanging from it?"

* * *

There was nothing as beautiful as a wintry scene after a departing blizzard. Dash blinked at the giant snowdrifts that had blown around the convention center. There was plenty of snow for snowball fights, tobogganing, and making snowmen. They could have a snow-family contest near the international bazaar, and all the purchased clothing used to decorate the snow-families could be donated to the homeless shelter.

The tall trees surrounding Southside Glen were laden with thick clumps of snow, their branches drooping under the weight, and crystal icicles hung down naturally. They could have a Christmas tree decorating contest. That would spur sales of ornaments and craft supplies. Perhaps the profits could be donated to the vocational school. What an idea.

"You seem to be full of wonder," Misty said while she drove through the complex. "I'm sure the convention centers in San Francisco are bigger."

He shook his head. While the Cow Palace was huge, it wasn't size that mattered. This place had charm. He spotted a frozen pond right outside the giant dome where the Christmas tree stood and pointed excitedly.

"Oh, that's where the water main broke," Misty said. "I'm sure Mr. Weston will want it cleaned up. It ruined the flowerbeds."

Dash shook his head and made gestures, pumping his arms like he was ice-skating. Who cared about flowerbeds in the deep of winter?

"Are you thinking what I'm thinking?" Misty grinned, her blue eyes sparkling.

He bobbed his head up and down in a fierce nod, then pointed to the huge piles of snow and the surrounding trees, sparkling with ice crystals.

"Oh, Sam! You're brilliant. We can have the North Pole part of the village out here. I know Mr. Weston wanted everything indoors because he doesn't want anyone to leave Southside and end up in the center of town, but we're still far enough away from the town square that the visitors would likely stay put."

Those were the objectives of having a grand indoors experience, but Dash was more interested in the overall profits which equaled revenues minus costs. It wouldn't do to have the "perfect" indoor experience if the costs were jacked up and they ended up losing money despite a big turnout.

He made big gestures with his hands, trying to convey that whoever this Mr. Weston was, he would certainly approve of huge piles of money. He even drew a dollar sign with his finger and made like he was carrying big bags of money.

"You're so funny," Misty said. "I'll propose your idea to Gordon and see if he wants to pass it on to Mr. Weston."

Dash nodded eagerly and enjoyed the rest of the drive over hill and down dale through snow-covered meadows and by frosty forests to the Jolly Ranch just west of town square. This inside scoop was worth his weight in gold, and he couldn't wait to see how tricked out the Jolly Ranch would be. After all, Nick Jolly the First was a set decorator for all the old black-and-white Christmas movies while Nick Jolly the Second did the animatronics for the flying reindeer for movies made before computer-generated graphics.

Misty turned the corner over an unplowed road and through a giant archway made from a huge redwood stump. Bright neon lights twinkled, announcing the words, "Welcome to Jolly Ranch, where Christmas reigns supreme."

A prancing sleigh drawn by dashing and dancing reindeer moved up and down as if flying above the two-story-high stump. It was laden with a covering of snow, but two men were perched on stepladders, busy brushing it off.

Misty waved to them. "Those are my brothers, Nick the third, and Rick, the one with the Waldo glasses."

Dash wanted to say he definitely did not look like Waldo, but then, he couldn't blow his cover—not yet. He nodded and waved back at the brothers. They were both wearing Christmas lumberjack outfits, with red-and-green-checkered shirts, trousers with suspenders, and heavy boots.

The ranch-style house was long and sprawling, decorated to the eaves with twinkling lights entwined in dark-green garlands wrapped around every bush and pole. A snow-family lined the path to the front door, and Dash easily spotted the one which represented Misty. She was wearing a hot-pink ski jacket, pink earmuffs, and had a tangled brown nest of hair, a carrot nose, and sky-blue eyes. What made her stand apart was her stick arms, one up and the other down, as if she were dashing through the snow.

"Woof, woof, woof!" Westie barked, prancing on his lap with his nose pressed against the window. He was complaining about the lack of a little dog like him.

"Woo, grrr, ruff, yip," Dash said, meaning, "Patience, patience, little guy. You have to worm your way into a woman's heart, not push."

"Wwwhir, grrr, yap, yap," Westie said. "You might be a worm, but I'm a West Highland terrier, and I'm more Christmassy than that Alaskan malamute."

The giant husky came barreling out the door, followed by the nasty tomcat named Figgy who jumped onto a porch rail and arched his back in a most unwelcoming manner.

"We're here!" Misty trilled in a cheery tone. "Mom! Dad! You won't believe what happened. I caused a plane crash and rescued a man from freezing to death."

She ran around the Jeep and opened the door for Dash before he could decide how to approach the Jolly couple. Misty's father, Nick the Second, was as rotund and jolly-looking as the Coca-Cola Santa. His beard was thick and white, and he wore round wire-rimmed glasses. He wasn't dressed in a Santa suit—no one would for a family dinner, and suddenly, Dash wondered if he was overdressed. What was he thinking wearing a suit and top hat?

Mrs. Jolly was wearing an apron over what looked like a Victorian era dress of dark-green velvet. Her eyes were bright blue, like Misty's, and her cheeks were pink and pretty, again like her daughter. Her smile beamed like searchlights when he alighted from the Jeep.

"You came for dinner!" Her arms surrounded Misty's thin frame with a big, wide hug. "And you brought a guest."

"This is the man who crashed his plane. He's a dentist named Dr. Sam Finnegan, but we call him Sam Single, because he was dressed like Kris Kringle's little brother. He's going to be the Santa for Christmas Village. What a good sport," Misty said at a speed-talking pace without taking a breath.

"Whoa there, slow down there, hold them horses, Missy Misty." Mr. Jolly held his belly and laughed, turning toward Dash.

"Ho, ho, ho. We heard all about the crash from Brad. He's still there investigating. Glad you're not hurt too badly."

"Come on in, Dr. Finnegan," Mrs. Jolly said. "You must have had quite a day."

"It's wrrr, yap, woof," Dash said, hurriedly remembering to make dog sounds.

"Oh, Mom and Dad, I forgot to tell you, but Dr. Finnegan is in shock from the crash. He's lost his voice, and it's all my fault for driving on the runway. You see, he was flying in even though the airport is closed. I bet he didn't see that there was no one in the control tower, and well, he barely missed landing on my Jeep. The hood's dented, and it's lucky I hit the brakes or I would have been runway pancake."

"Wwwaooof, waar, roofff." Westie barked to warn Dash he'd better turn off Misty's yap before she shined too much light on the airplane and why a dentist would be flying into a blizzard.

Dash smoothly placed his arm around Misty's shoulders and gave her a kiss on the side of her head.

"Is something going on here?" Misty's mother crooned. "Oh my, well, come on in. No use standing out here in the cold. I'm Grace and this is my husband, Nick. You might have driven by my sons, Nick and Rick, out front. No doubt you're going to get all of us confused, but don't you worry."

"There will be a quiz." Misty's father gave Dash a hearty handshake. "I hear you're a dentist. Our town's been missing a dentist ever since old Dr. Loisel retired and moved to Florida."

Dash shrank underneath Mr. Jolly's steely gaze, as if he were interrogating an imposter. Before he could respond, or not respond, since he was "in shock," Misty came to his rescue.

"Oh, Dad, let's not bore Sam with all of your toothaches. You really ought to take better care of your teeth."

"Kind of hard to lay off the sweets when your mom's such a talented baker," Mr. Jolly retorted.

"Aaarf, aww, woof." Westie licked his chops at the mouthwatering smell of roasting meat. He was clearly looking forward to the accidental drops from the table.

Dash's nose was inexplicably sensitive enough to pick out the dish—roast beef with parsnips, carrots, and English mustard, nice and strong. Elsewhere, the scent of pine, cinnamon, cedar, and roasting chestnuts hit him with Christmas overload, and the decor was as posh as a department store window.

A fully decked-out Christmas tree was laden with ornaments, large and small, dressed with strings of lights, and streaked with tinsel. Every horizontal surface held pine cones and garlands, intertwined with ribbons and twinkle lights in between miniature gingerbread houses, Christmas-themed lighthouses, cottages, sleighs, and castles. A model railroad wound its way around the base of the Christmas tree, and a Christmas train filled with elves and animals chugged on the tracks, making a circuit every few minutes.

Christmas songs played from the surround sound speakers, not loud enough to interfere with conversation, and tiny bells tinkled from the abundantly packed wreaths over every door, not to mention generous sprigs of mistletoe beneath every doorway and dangling from the open beams of the ceiling.

Misty unwrapped Dash's scarf and took his suit jacket. "Let's get some of those cookies hot out of the oven. Mom doesn't care if we spoil our appetite. In fact, she believes cookies are the best appetizer—especially hers. After my grandmother passed last year, I'll have to agree, but don't tell her that Granny snuck us cookies before dinner, too. Double sugar high!"

Dash grinned at the naughtiness of stealing cookies in front of her parents. Westie wriggled excitedly, but when he stepped into the kitchen a loud hiss and a pounce of gray-striped fur startled him.

Figgy dropped right on top of him. Westie let out an outraged yelp, which Dash understood as, "Scat cat. You fat brat."

The tabby tomcat hissed and spat, showing his claws, and a tall man wearing reindeer antlers over his mop of brown hair grabbed the cat before he could rip Westie's silk cape off.

"Sorry about that," he said, curling the cat into the crook of his arm. "Figgy doesn't like small animals. He wasn't always like this, at least not in the nineteenth century, but once he traveled to our time, she turned into a he, and well, he's a spunky boy, this one."

"Oh, don't mind my brother, Mick," Misty said. "He's had quite a shock two years back. Thinks he traveled back in time and met Figgy when he was a she."

Mick extended a hand to Dash. "I hear you dropped out of the sky. Say, you're dressed like a bloke from an old black-and-white Christmas movie."

Dash shook his hand while staring at the outlandish sweater Mick wore. It had an appliqué of a headless woodsman chopping down a Christmas tree while an old-fashioned lady stood by.

Mick held on to Dash's hand and shook longer than proper, as if he was on to something. When he let go, he winked and gave the cat a knowing look.

What was that about? Did the cat tell him something about Dash?

"Well, Mick, where's Kitty?" Misty asked in a chirpy voice. "I see her cat got home, but is she coming to dinner?"

"Kitty's babysitting for Dr. Dale," Mick said. "He's having nanny troubles."

"I thought Merry was helping out." Everyone in town heard about Dr. Dale's nanny, Tamara Scott, leaving Dottie unsupervised, and how Merry found her near the icy creek while she was delivering the mail.

"Dr. Dale doesn't want Dottie to get too attached to any one babysitter. Not after Tamara flaked out." Mick glanced furtively at the kitchen where Merry was helping their mother. "He also doesn't want Merry to get too attached to him."

"Oh, really? How do you know?" Misty asked.

"I'm male. I read body language. Dr. Dale can't keep his eyes off Merry, but he refuses to smile when she's around. You could be laughing and joking with him, and in walks Merry and he clams up."

"Wow, so little Merry is secretly falling in love without letting on."

"It's not wise to let anyone know—not in this nosy family."

"Don't you hear things at the post office?" Misty waggled a finger at him. "Come on, spill what you know."

"You'll have to ask Kitty since she's at the counter all day. I don't hear anything out delivering mail in a blizzard." Mick speared Dash an inquisitive glance. "How's the project going at Southside?"

"We've only three days before opening Christmas Village," Misty noted. "We have to do December 20, 21, and 22 as if it was December 23, 24, and 25. Then do it again on the 23, 24, and 25, and again on the 26, 27, 28. Three complete Christmas Experience Episodes with three tree lightings, three Gala Balls, three Christmas Eve fairs, and three Christmas Day sock hops."

"Why don't you combine the second one with the real one at the town square?" Mick asked. "That'll save you the duplication. Plus, if you want Dad to sit on Santa's throne, he can't be at two places at the same time."

"Oh, we really can't," Misty said. "The Christmas Village Inn and all the hotels at the convention center are booked solid. Those guests are expecting a tightly coordinated experience. Mr. Weston wants to maximize profits, so we can't have any spillover to the town square."

"Why, that's abominably selfish of him," Mick interjected. "Why can't we share the business? He expects people to travel through our roads, use our airport and gas stations and then only spend money at Southside Glen?"

Misty shrugged and arranged several chocolate chunk and peppermint cookies on a platter. "He's the main investor, and it's between him and Gordon. My job is to make sure the events are fully staffed, scheduled, and smoothly run—no hiccups. Here, have a cookie."

Dash cringed at how vehement Misty's brother sounded. He'd done his research. If anything, the gas stations should be happy at the amount of traffic his Christmas Village would bring. And if people didn't want to freeze their tushes off at the town square or fight for parking at the swimming hole turned ice pond, they would naturally stick around Southside and spend their money at a clean, convenient, and well-coordinated venue with multilevel parking.

"Don't mind my brother," Misty whispered as she fed him a delectably sweet peppermint and chocolate chunk cookie. "Oops. I hope I'm not giving you a cavity."

Dash thoroughly enjoyed the cookie and gave Misty a hug, rubbing his nose with hers after licking the crumbs off her lips. There was so much he wanted to say to her, but for now, it was better to observe in silence. His father had built his retail empire on mystery shopping, and Dash was going to corner the Christmas market by being the most mysterious Santa ever.

Chapter Ten

Dinner was pleasant and Misty noticed *Sam* enjoying himself despite being left out of the conversation. Her brothers were naturally suspicious of him, and Mick provoked him repeatedly, asking if it was okay to eat a sweet or bite down on a nut.

To *Sam's* credit, he only politely smiled and proceeded to eat the sweet and crunch down on the nut in question, eliciting friendly smiles from everyone else.

"Hey, now that Misty's here with a date, let's go ice-skating at Swimmer's Hole so she can hold his hand," Mick said at the dinner table after everyone had feasted on the roast and vegetables.

"I'm so stuffed, I don't think I can skate to the couch," Misty said. "Besides, I'm not sure Sam should ice skate since he might be suffering from a head injury."

"We're due for the caroling marathon tonight," Mom reminded everyone. "We almost have all our voices here. Misty and Merry's soprano and Holly and Ivy's alto. Nick and Mick's bass, and Rick's baritone. Sam, what range do you sing?"

"Mom! Sam had a shock. I'm sure he'll be happy to lip-sync, won't you?" Misty flashed *Sam* a hopeful look while Gordon glared at the dentist as if he were one giant sore tooth. Why was Gordon so hostile to poor ol' *Sam*?

"Don't mind Gordon," Misty whispered to *Sam*. "He's just grouchy because of his raging toothache. Maybe you can look at it sometime."

Sam shrugged but nodded agreeably, wearing a silly smile, so Misty leaned forward and kissed him. It was special of Mom to ask *Sam* to be included in family caroling, especially since Gordon was a reformed Grinch and said he couldn't carry a tune, and Ivy's boyfriend, Brad, was always too busy as the lone town sheriff. Not that Misty was in "competition" with her sisters on who had the best boyfriend. But still, *Sam* would fit in with the family since he was an obvious Christmas lover. He would also be a welcome addition to the town which was filled with sweet-toothed folks, resulting in plenty of toothaches needing dental work.

But she was getting ahead of herself so she kissed him again and snuggled against his side.

"Arf, ruff," Westie barked from underneath the table, reminding her of where her affection should be.

"Oh, let's bring the puppy," Merry said. "I know a little girl who wants a puppy for Christmas."

Misty scooped Westie from underneath the table. He was busy gobbling up a big fat hunk of meat while *Sam* looked at the ceiling, acting innocent.

"Sam's adopting this one," Misty said. "The two of them have a bond."

"It wouldn't hurt to let Dottie pet him," Merry said. "Where did you find him? Maybe he already has an owner."

"He's a superdog, flying across the driven snow," Misty said. "And no, he has no collar or tags."

"The dog comes with us," Dad pronounced. "Since he's a stray, he's good luck, just like Figgy was good luck for Mick."

Rudolph, Holly's Alaskan malamute, didn't want to be left out of the picture, so he raised his head and howled.

"That's our second baritone," Holly said, fluffing the dog's mane. "You don't have to be a stray to bring good luck. Just ask Gordie."

Gordon swallowed antacid and groaned at the reference to Rudolph's role in inviting him back into the mansion that first Gala Ball when he was on the outside looking in. It was hard to believe the arrogant and bossy Gordon Gills had once been somewhat of a "stray."

"Sam's not a stray," Misty said. "And he brought good luck to our Christmas Village already."

"How so?" Gordon sneered as he stabbed his serving of plum pudding.

"Why, he found the solution to our snow problem," Misty said. "We have sky-high snowdrifts right outside the domed area, and when Sam saw the frozen water over the flowerbeds, he thought we could have the ice-skating pond right there."

"Mr. Weston won't agree to it," Gordon said. "He was adamant about the complete experience being indoors. It's all about the package and the wrapping. No loose ends."

"I know, but he's not going to like the cost overruns either," Misty said. "Why can't the visitors step outside for a breather to enjoy our natural snow and ice?"

"Mr. Weston specifically stated that he wants all of *his* visitors to stay put at Southside Glen with no spillover to the town," Gordon argued. "Once they step outdoors for sledding, they might want to explore the rest of the vicinity."

"What? That's horrible. Why can't we share the visitors?" Mom interrupted. "I'm sure some of our longtime visitors will be curious enough to go to his Christmas Village. Why can't the tourists staying at the convention center visit us here?"

"They can, but we have to ensure that they're so busy, they won't want to leave," Gordon explained. "We sunk in so much money, we have to make a profit."

"Mr. Weston seems awfully selfish," Mick said, reiterating his criticism.

Misty hated that they were talking business at her family table, especially with a guest present. "Let's table this and talk about this tomorrow. I'm sure Sam here has no interest in our behind-the-scenes business."

Sam appeared to be studying the depths of his coffee cup while slipping food scraps to Westie underneath the table.

"You can blow it off because you're not the one responsible," Gordon sniffed. "I'm the one who has to deal with Dastardly Dash Weston. The airport is open again, and I want to be available to pick him up."

"Maybe he's not coming," Misty said. "Why don't you worry about it tomorrow?"

"Ah, maybe you're right." Gordon pushed from the table. "His secretary says he hasn't checked in with her. Probably trolled us into thinking he was coming and made us worried for nothing."

"I'm sure we'll pull it all together by opening day," Misty said. "Mom, Dad, want to drop by tomorrow and see the progress? The vendors will be filling their booths, and we're getting the petting zoo ready for the animals. The tree will be ready for lighting, and Constanza has the bed and breakfast not just looking scrumptious and smelling like a candy store, but fully decorated with every pillow fluffed and breakfast ready to be served. Sam's the lucky guy who already got the first night stay."

"We might just drop by," Dad said. "But tonight, let's show your young man the way Christmas is done at Christmas Creek. Ho, ho, ho, on a four-horse open sleigh."

"We need that many horses for our big family," Misty explained. "What are we waiting for? Let's go."

* * *

It was all Dash could do to control his emotions while watching Gordon trash Misty's idea about using the iced-over flowerbed for the skating rink. The way he acted so dismissive of her made him what to punch him in the nose.

But Dash was a professional mystery shopper, and while in data gathering mode, he needed to keep on the down-low. He swallowed his indignation and fed scraps to Westie who was giving his own opinion about the charade.

"Whirr, wrruff, woof," Westie said, meaning, "No offense to you, *Sam*, but I don't want you to adopt me. Misty found me, so I should go with her. It's the finders keepers rule."

Dash couldn't counter the argument without making doggy sounds, so he picked up Westie and ruffled his silky head, pissing off the puppy even more.

"I'm telling you, Misty is a gem. You better not mess this up. She thinks you're Sam the dentist. What is she going to do when she finds out you're the Dastardly Dash Weston, Christmas hater galore?" The little dog made rumbling noises punctuated by tiny yips and yaps.

Dash held Westie close and pretended to kiss his head while making tiny sounds. "Don't worry about me. If Misty likes the silent Sam, she'll be charmed by the real me."

"Really? The guy who hates all things Christmas is going to win over Miss Christmas herself?"

"Sam?" Misty's voice sounded amused. "What are you and Westie whispering about? Are you feeling better after your shock?"

"Arrf, warf, wow," Westie said, urging Dash to fess up about his identity.

Instead, Dash smiled silently at Misty and handed Westie to her. He turned his attention to the plum cake dessert and ate it with gusto, even though he hated Christmas fruitcake and its gooey ilk. This one was not so bad, but still, it was only okay during the Yuletide like his other nemesis, mincemeat pie.

Westie did have a point. The way to win over Misty was through Christmas, but once she loved him, she would understand why silly and frivolous Christmas stuff rubbed him the wrong way, unless it was to make a buck or two or more. Heh, heh.

"Ready?" Misty petted Westie and extended a smile to Dash once everyone had finished dessert. "Have you ever been in a four-horse sleigh?"

Dash shook his head.

"Are you excited?"

Dash nodded.

"Great. You'll have to sit by me in the back row."

He raised his eyebrows in question.

She cupped her hand and whispered, "So no one can see what we're doing underneath the blanket."

He made an O with his mouth and she giggled, taking his hand.

Westie yapped, "I'll know."

Dash felt like growling, but he restrained himself. He was only going along with the Jolly family to get ideas for the Christmas Village concept. Putting on a smile, he helped Mrs. Jolly clear the table while the rest of the family went to change into their Christmas outfits.

Mr. Jolly, predictably, emerged in a full Santa suit, complete with red jacket, pants, and a big belt. The brothers were lumberjacks and hunters with red-and-green-checkered jackets and hats, each dangling mistletoe over the brim. Holly was a cross between an elf and a fairy, wearing the traditional elf dress and shoes but with the addition of gossamer wings and a silver wand. Ivy was a sparkly ice princess with a full tiara of crystals, and Merry dressed as a doll with two red dots on her cheeks, a pigtailed wig, and a gingham frock underneath her patchwork coat.

Misty wore a red velvet dress with white trim, but was not as decked out as the others. She'd probably toned it down because he wasn't wearing a costume, and she didn't want him to feel out of place. Gordon wasn't dressed in anything unusual, just a rancher's coat over jeans, and of course, everyone lamented that Ivy's boyfriend, the sheriff, was busy directing traffic.

Together, they set off from the ranch house toward the barn. The family was full of chitchat and horsing around, and Dash couldn't help feeling like he'd missed something growing up. The brothers pushed and shoved each other around, laughing and joking, while the sisters giggled and tittered and teased their mother for wearing the previous year's themed outfit instead of going all out as Mrs. Claus.

Misty was a worthwhile hostess, showing him around the barn and introducing him to each of the four horses as her father and brothers got them tacked up and ready for the sleigh.

The sleigh itself was a wondrous and magical-looking vehicle. It was covered with glitter and crystals, like it was made of sparkling ice. Dash had expected something painted red and green, but he could see how the ice crystal look would magnify the fantasy of being in a bejeweled winter wonderland.

Misty and her sisters took selfies and pictures with him and Westie, and once they boarded the sleigh and the horses trotted off with sleigh bells ringing, Dash felt like he was transported into a fairy tale. Misty snuggled with him underneath a heavy woolen blanket while Westie, who didn't mind the cold, perched himself on Misty's lap with his forepaws on the back of the sleigh. Dash turned to see what the puppy was looking at and caught his breath at the sheer beauty. Ice sparkled off the trees, and the winding trail left by the sleigh and hooves in the freshly fallen snow looked like a scene from a greeting card.

It brought back memories of his dear mother writing Christmas cards while he picked up the glitter that fell from the cards with his finger and rubbed them onto a window so he could see them wink and sparkle in the filtered sunlight. He'd never understood snow at Christmas or the appeal—not as a city boy where the Christmas tree in Union Square was sprayed with fake snow, and the skating rink was well-groomed and bordered with concrete, and the twinkle lights were wound around bulky palm trees instead of stately fir trees.

Out here, in the moonlight, with the nippy air and the happy sounds of family, but especially with a sweet woman cuddled against him, all Dash wanted was to capture the moment forever. He sharpened his senses, immersing himself in the scent of Misty, the wool, and the crisp stinging breeze, the sounds of the sleigh runners swishing, and the jingling of the sleigh bells, and the warmth of being included for the ride.

No one owed him anything, least of all Misty, but the Jolly family had extended their hand of friendship while he was there under false pretenses. Yet, if he blew his cover now, he'd be thrown off the sleigh and left out in the cold—on the outside looking in, an old miserly man staring at his profit and loss spreadsheet.

Westie jumped on his lap and licked him but gave him no advice.

He petted the dog with one hand and put his arm around Misty, drawing her in tighter, wishing the ride would last forever.

The town square came into view all too soon, and Dash couldn't keep his eyes off the majestic Christmas tree that soared to the sky. It had to be at least three times higher than the artificial tree they had under the dome, and it was firmly rooted to the earth.

Colorful lights and shiny ornaments bedazzled the tree, and the star up top was more magnificent than he'd pictured.

"It's gorgeous, isn't it?" Misty said. "Handmade by a local craftsperson. I believe this one was made by one of the residents living in the homeless shelter."

Dash noticed throngs of people walking up and down the sidewalks. He couldn't tell if they were locals or tourists, but everyone was obviously dressed warmly, and clumps of people broke out in Christmas songs on a spontaneous basis.

A cheer roared out when the Jolly sleigh approached a series of lights with markings like a runway and banner strung across a wire proclaiming it as "Santa's landing spot."

"Ho, ho, ho!" Mr. Jolly bellowed, standing up at the front of the sleigh and waving to the crowd. "Ho, ho, ho! Welcome, welcome to Christmas Creek."

Dash wasn't sure what he was supposed to do, but all the rest of the Jollys waved to people on both sides of the sleigh. He stuck out like a sore thumb and wished he could hide under the blanket.

"Wave to them," Misty prompted. "You're a part of this year's Christmas festivities. You're Sam Single, Kris Kringle's little brother, and you're reigning at Christmas Village this year."

Dash wanted to argue that this wasn't Christmas Village, and no one knew him, and what if they wouldn't wave back, or even worse, threw eggs and tomatoes at him, but grinning like his teeth were frozen, Dash waved to no one in particular.

Soon people gathered at the base of the giant Christmas tree. Friends and neighbors greeted each other warmly and caught up on the gossip. Everyone seemed genuinely happy to be out in the freezing weather so soon after a blizzard had swept through.

Some came on snowmobiles while others trudged on cross-country skis and snowshoes, dragging sleds full of children. Many of the pickup trucks had snowplow attachments, and they made the way for the rest of the hardy people.

Team leaders bearing signs gathered people into caroling groups based on theme or musical genre: classic carols, bluesy folk songs, rocking Christmas beats, children's favorites, Spanish-language, and traditional hymns.

The mayor spoke, and then Gordon spoke. He invited everyone to check out the opening day of Christmas Village at Southside Glen and called on Misty to come to the podium.

Dash reluctantly let go of Misty's hand, but she tugged his sleeve. "Come with me. We're going to introduce you as the Southside Santa."

He wanted to ask if they'd checked with Mr. Weston, but that would be stupid. Of course they hadn't, because *he* was Mr. Weston.

The townsfolk greeted him with a warm welcome, and Dash couldn't place the sense of belonging, even though he was a stranger to town.

Misty took the microphone from Gordon and said, "I can't wait for all of you to come to our brand-new Christmas Village at Southside. We'll have many surprises for you."

"Tell us, tell us," the teenagers gathered in the front shouted. "What surprises?"

"Can't tell you or it won't be a surprise," Misty said. "But I'll let you in on a secret."

She leaned closer to the audience and cupped her mouth as if she were going to whisper.

"Tell us the secret," the crowd demanded.

Misty put her arm over Dash's shoulders and pushed him forward. "I found us a dentist. He literally dropped out of the sky right at my feet. Folks, I'd like you to meet Dr. Sam Finnegan. Let's go all out to make sure Sam enjoys his stay at Christmas Creek and persuade him to set up practice here. With all the sweets we eat, we do need a man like Sam."

"What's the surprise?" a teen girl asked, followed by the townspeople chanting, "No secrets," followed by, "We need a dentist."

"We do, but the secret is, we need to be nice to Sam and show him how hospitable we are at Christmas Creek, and..." She dragged out her words, seemingly for suspense.

The crowd fell silent, hanging on to her every word.

Beaming confidently, she continued. "You'll find out if you drop by Santa's Gazebo at Christmas Village, opening this coming Monday, December twentieth. Southside Glen. Be there, and don't be square."

"We will!" the crowd responded excitedly.

Dash had to wonder at how talented she was at working a crowd. Was she even aware of her gift? He gave a hearty wave but couldn't muster it within himself to say, "Ho, ho, ho." Then again, he might have embarrassed himself and ended up barking like a wild dog. That would be a surprise!

Chapter Eleven

Misty sang her voice raw as she and her family went door to door, entertaining the townsfolk with their Christmas carols. *Sam* was such a good sport, tagging along and even wiggling his butt to "Rockin' Around the Christmas Tree." Even though he had no voice, his lip-syncing had everyone fooled.

"You're just a jolly good fellow." Misty nudged *Sam*. "I'm so glad you dropped in early even though we weren't ready."

"Last stop," Dad announced, pulling the sleigh to the end of a snowy lane. "There's a vacant house next door where ol' Dr. Loisel used to live."

Misty nudged *Sam* again, but she said nothing because she didn't want to put pressure on him. Still, he must have been interested enough in Christmas Creek to come early and book a stay at Southside. He'd even braved a blizzard to get to town, and he was carefully studying and marveling at every sight and sound he encountered. She saw how long he stared at the general store which was not only painted to look like a gingerbread house, but had packages of candy and cookies tacked to the walls and hanging from the rafters.

He'd also looked behind every bush and traced the wires for the animatronics display her brother set up at the mayor's house and the competing one at the fire chief's house, complete with an antique fire truck draped with evergreens and lights.

Sam also spotted a furniture store and marveled at the antiques he could see through the window. He was especially curious about a heavy wooden throne carved with holly leaves and ivy around the trim.

"Now that would be a magnificent throne for Santa," Misty said. "Unfortunately, it's way over budget."

Thankfully Gordon had begged off from the caroling, saying he had to contact Mr. Weston and run some numbers. Otherwise, he would have accused *Sam* of snooping around the townsfolks' Christmas decorations. What was wrong with her sister's bossy boyfriend? It wasn't as if *Sam* was competition for best Jolly boyfriend, or was he?

"Like what you see?" Mom said to *Sam* when they passed Dr. Loisel's empty house. "The dentist left his chairs behind. We always figured a new one would fall in love with this sweet-as-pie town."

Sam grinned and nodded, walking around the house to survey it. By the time he returned, Misty and her family were finished visiting Mrs. Wing's house.

"Let's be sure to go by Dr. Dale's house," Merry shouted to her father. "I'm sure Dottie would be glad to see us."

"Kitty, too," Mick reminded everyone of his girlfriend who had to babysit tonight. "Guess I'll have to go to game night alone since she's busy babysitting."

"Maybe Dr. Dale is back," Merry said.

Mick shook his head, looking at his phone. "Kitty just texted me saying Dr. Dale got a call to deliver Bella and Chance's baby."

"My stars," Mom said. "I sure hope it's an easy delivery. With Bella's cerebral palsy, how is she supposed to push?"

"That's why Colton has to be there," Merry said.

"Is it Colton now and not Dr. Dale?" Misty teased as Dad pulled the sleigh up to Dr. Dale's house near the creek. Westie barked and whined like he wanted to butt into the conversation, so Misty palmed the wiggly puppy off to Merry.

"I'm only calling him Colton because of Dottie." Merry let the puppy lick her face, even though she was made up to be a doll and sported two large red splotches on her cheeks and fake freckles. "We can let Dottie pet Westie when we drop by. She wants a dog so badly, but her father isn't sure she knows how to take care of one."

"No better time than to learn with someone else's dog," Misty said with a wink. "Maybe Westie can spend the night with Dottie."

"Does this mean Kitty could be gone all night?" Mick asked, sounding disappointed while Misty studied her twin sister. She was definitely up to something, so animated whenever she spoke about Dr. Dale—even calling him Colton. Was she in love?

"Poor Colton," Merry said as they walked up the path to the doctor's house. "He fired the nanny, and he can't find another one so close to Christmas."

"Tamara had to go," Mom said. "Imagine letting that poor child run loose down the street. If you hadn't found her..."

"It's lucky I was delivering the mail and saw her fallen down near the creek," Merry said. "Maybe I'll switch places with Kitty so she and Mick can go to game night at the Pinecone."

"Are you sure it's okay with Dr. Dale to switch babysitters?" Misty asked. "I heard he didn't want you always to be sole babysitter."

"That's because Dottie's always asking for me, and he doesn't want her to get hurt. I would never hurt her, but after Tamara left, I guess he has to be careful."

"Right, so you're pushing your luck." Why did it always fall on Misty to rein in her clueless twin?

"Kitty deserves some time off, and I can handle Dr. Dale," Merry said. "The poor man is overworked and needs looking after."

"I wonder why you're looking after him." Ivy giggled and messed with Merry's fishhook-shaped pigtails. Misty cast an appraising glance at her twin. Was it the effect of the bright-red dots painted on her cheeks or was she blushing underneath it all? If so, Merry could be hiding a secret crush on the doctor. She was aiming high for sure. Wow!

Misty held her arm around *Sam's* waist and leaned closer to him. At least her man wasn't keeping her at arm's length, even though she'd ruined his private plane.

"Merry, is there something you're not telling us?" Holly jibed with a sneaky smile on her face. "Could it be you're too quiet?"

Merry shook her head so vehemently, her dangling pigtails slapping her face. "I was only trying to help. It's not fair that Kitty has to stay all night now that Dr. Dale might be delayed with delivering the baby."

"You never know how long a baby takes," Mom hooted. "I didn't know Chance and Bella's baby was due."

"It's a little early." Merry's brow furrowed. "But she'll be in good hands with Dr. Dale."

"I'm sure his hands are quite good," Holly teased, causing Merry's entire face to turn red.

"Ho, ho, ho, and here we are a-caroling." Dad ended the teasing by knocking on Dr. Dale's door. Westie dashed up the porch steps and squeezed himself between Dad's boots.

Kitty opened the door with a big smile on her face. "I have cookies and hot apple cider. Come on in."

Dottie peeked from behind Kitty, and her eyes grew as large as saucers. "Is that my puppy? He's a superdog with a red cape."

"Why, Dottie, it's not Christmas yet," Merry replied. "And you haven't replied to Gramma Frost's last letter."

Misty had a moment when she wondered how Merry would know, but Dottie's antics amused her too much.

Westie was pawing at the screen door, barking in friendly yips, begging to be let in.

"Dad's too busy to help me," Dottie said. "Can you?"

"Of course, I can. I bet Gramma Frost is looking in her empty mailbox." Merry opened the child-sized mailbox she installed on Dr. Dale's porch and looked inside, but there were no letters.

"Don't just stand there," Kitty said, holding a tray of steamy drinks. "Come on in."

Westie was the first to charge in and jump into Dottie's welcoming arms. He was all over her, licking and wiggling like the cutie he was.

"Are you sure it's okay for Dottie to touch the dog?" Mom asked.

Merry had already told the family why Dr. Dale was skeptical of pets. He was a widower, and his dear departed wife had allergies. He was afraid Dottie might have inherited the allergies, but as Misty had pointed out, there was no better time to find out than with someone else's pet. Misty darted a glance at *Sam* to see how he was taking it.

Sam shrugged and made like he didn't care if Westie went with the girl. Hmmm, maybe Misty was being too bossy in tagging

Westie for the dentist. She'd been told she tried too hard and made too many assumptions, but so far, *Silent Sam* hadn't said 'no' to any of her ideas.

Once the family crowded into the cozy living room, they linked arms and sang, "There's No Place Like Home for the Holidays."

Misty pointed at *Sam* lip-syncing with gusto, and behind his back, she made the time-out sign. It was a signal her family knew all too well because the joke had been played on each one of them—sort of a rite of initiation.

As they closed in on the last words, everyone other than *Sam* turned toward Misty to wait for the signal, and then right at the very end, when they were supposed to do the final "home, sweet HOOOME" the Jollys held their breath in unison, leaving *Sam* to howl all alone, "Hooooooo!!!!"

Sam had his hands spread wide, his chest out, and his face lifted on that last high note. When he realized he was alone and out there, he clapped both hands over his mouth and dropped to his knees, staring back at Misty and blinking like a deer caught in the headlamps.

Misty burst out laughing, and soon, she was rolling on the floor holding on to *Sam* who goodness-to-gracious was also laughing. This was as good as it got. A boyfriend who didn't talk back, who loved Christmas, and had a fantastic sense of humor.

* * *

The first thing Dash did after Misty dropped him off at Mrs. Claus's was ask to borrow her computer. Westie had stayed at Dr. Dale's place for a "sleepover" to test if the little darling had allergies, and Misty of course had to go home so she could be up in the morning to supervise the vendors coming in and stocking their stores and displays. It was going to be a hectic day, but Dash had to take charge before Gordon drove everything into the ground.

Misty was the event planner, and she was doing a great job as far as he was concerned. She didn't need the constant criticism and micromanaging from Gordon. Dash had to correct this before it got worse. He could see the stress and strain Misty was under and how she tried hard to mitigate the damage.

In fact, his heart swelled when Misty gave a plug for Christmas Village in front of the town square. As far as he was concerned, Misty should be in charge of everything and Gordon, who was rumored to be a reformed Grinch, should go away.

Dash booted up Mrs. Claus's computer and navigated to his email.

Egads! The box was overflowing with messages. Darlene, his assistant, not secretary, what an archaic term, was worried about the plane crash. Apparently, the Christmas Creek sheriff had run a check on the identification numbers coming from his plane's transponder and was asking for him, Mr. Weston, to confirm if he'd filed a flight plan or had his airplane stolen.

As usual, the sheriff wasn't naming names. Police never gave away what they knew and always kept back details in order to trap people who were lying.

Dash decided not to answer. He didn't want Sam to be in trouble, nor did he want to clue Gordon in that he was the dreaded or dastardly Dash Weston. Humpf. Let the sheriff waste his time investigating. He'd get nothing out of Sam who was supposedly still in shock and completely silent.

He turned to Gordon's emails. The man had no judgment and common sense. What was he thinking of paying a standing around fee for the lazy contractor who left in the middle of a blizzard? He'd bet that contractor hadn't been waiting anywhere.

A quick shout out to Mrs. Claus confirmed his suspicions.

"No one was here but my poor little self." The voluminous woman hovered over him, fanning her heaving breast. "I was stranded here by the blizzard and hoping someone would dig their way into the center."

After her operatics about the howling wind, the crashing of branches against the roof, and the rattling of the windows, Dash let her go back to the kitchen where she was preparing Christmas quiches for the morning meal.

He typed out his reply to Gordon.

Dear Mr. Gills, in answer to the overtime and "standing around" charges. A big NO! The contractor is milking you. Any charges above and beyond the signed contract comes out of your profits. As for the refrigerated truck moving snow in from outside. That is another NO! Let the visitors venture outside where I heard there are mountains of snowdrifts and a frozen pond over the flowerbeds. If they wander down to the town, so be it. I have it on good authority that the town is invited to Christmas Village. - Dash Weston

The next email had Dash blowing his whiskers.

Dear Mr. Weston, we have an issue with the Santa Claus Miss Jolly suggested. As you know, Miss Jolly was supposed to ask her father, Nick Jolly, to be the Christmas Village Santa. We went to the trouble to heat the gazebo and throne for Nick's old bones, but she's been unsuccessful in obtaining her father's services. Instead, she's suggesting a stray dentist who crashed his plane in our airport. This careless man didn't heed the signs that the airport was closed and barged in during the middle of a blizzard. He has completely enchanted Miss Jolly with his wily ways, playing on her insecurities and wish to compete with her more accomplished sisters, Holly and Ivy. This dentist is completely unsuited to be Santa. He's way too muscular and fit, although my muscles are bigger. If we wanted a muscular Santa, I could very well do it myself, but I'm in charge of this entire extravaganza and I can't be stuck in a stinky Santa suit— not that this imposter will be in a traditional suit. He's gotten himself in a red-and-white-striped sweater underneath a light-blue lederhosen and blue suede elf shoes. Miss Jolly went and announced him to be the Christmas Village Santa without permission. What I need you to do is issue a retraction and hire a big, fat Santa from San Francisco. I'm sure there are a few laid off from your department stores this year. - Gordon Gills, Executive Director of Southside Glen

Dash dashed back a curt reply.

Miss Jolly is in charge. If she got this dentist free of charge, more power to her. Anything else? Don't let your toothache make you grouchy. - Dash

Chapter Twelve

Misty was late getting up, and late to breakfast; in fact, she was so late, her sister was already gone with the Jeep to the post office. Great. Just great. The last person she wanted to call was Gordon to give her a lift to Southside Glen.

What to do? What to do?

She got dressed in a jiffy, pulling on anything she could find. Dragging on her pink parka and wrapping a hot-pink scarf around her neck, she punched the speed dial for Gordon, 944.

"9-1-1, what is your emergency?" It was Angela Wing, the Christmas Creek dispatcher.

"Oh, sorry. I meant to get Gordon. This is Misty."

"I know who you are. We have caller ID here," Angela said. "Wait. Don't hang up. You have yet to come in and give your statement about the plane crash."

"I don't have time. I'm running late and Merry took off with the Jeep. I have to get to Southside Glen and let the vendors in. The petting zoo folks are coming to measure the pens, and the muckers are spreading straw and bedding. The boys and girls club is painting the gingerbread doghouses, and I have to make sure everyone's gas and electricity is turned on. Oh, and Constanza's asking for a police escort for the family heirlooms she's putting up for the Gold Rush and Timber Baron display case. Think Brad can give me a speedy ride to Southside?"

"Cut. Cut. Cut," Angela blared. "You called 9-1-1 to ask my brother to chauffeur you to your job? He has real emergencies to deal with."

"Yes, but he needs to take my statement on the plane crash, and this is killing two birds with one stone."

"Fine. Fine. Fine. He's on his way to Southside anyway. Looks like there was a break-in at Santa's Gazebo."

"What? When did this happen? Why hasn't anyone notified me?"

"You can ask my brother on the way over. Be ready and listen for the siren. He's in a hurry."

"So am I. And thanks." Misty hung up the phone and immediately punched in 944 to get Gordon.

"What now?" Gordon's annoyed voice answered. "While you were sleeping late, I've been on the phone trying to find a real Santa to replace that dentist of yours. And then I get to Southside and find the heated throne missing."

"Do you have any suspects?"

"Your brothers," Gordon growled. "That toilet they replaced the throne with looks like the broken one in your parents' garage."

"Then why did you call the police? Brad's on his way to take your statement."

"Insurance purposes, you dimwit."

"Hey, no name-calling," Misty said.

Outside, the short wallop of a police siren sounded three times.

Misty dashed out of the apartment she and Merry shared, almost tripped down the stairs, and sprinted toward the police cruiser.

Out of breath, she said to Brad, "Gordon's on the phone. Forget about the Santa's throne. He thinks my brothers swapped it as a prank."

"No, no, no!" Gordon screamed so loud, Misty was sure Brad heard. "He needs to give me an official police report for the insurance claim."

"Gimme that." Brad grabbed Misty's phone and slapped it to his ear. "Filing a fraudulent claim is a crime. Brother-in-law-to-be or not. Now, I'm coming to take your statement."

"But the throne is still missing," Gordon's voice boomed. "And maybe Misty's brothers didn't take it. It could have been that sneaky dentist. Has anyone seen him around?"

Brad hung up, handed Misty's phone back to her, and put the police cruiser in gear. With a swish of tires, and a back spray of snow, he revved the engine and they hightailed it toward Southside. Best of all, he flicked on the siren and pushed other traffic out of the way.

"Yeehaw!" Misty squealed, loving the speed. She was screaming with so much delight that Brad couldn't get a word in about the plane crash—not until she had a chance to get her story straight with *Sam*. Perhaps he'd forget to mention she'd been driving on the runway. After all, he shouldn't have been trying to land in a blizzard. He could have killed her!

They arrived at the convention center in record time, and Misty was halfway out the door before the car stopped rolling. A pickup truck was unloading hay, and other box trucks were lined up with workers unloading goods. Misty waved and shouted encouragement to the vendors, but her first stop was Santa's Gazebo.

Gordon growled at her and pointed to the toilet. "Tell me you don't recognize that one."

"It looks like any other American Standard," Misty said. "How can you accuse my brothers when it could have been anyone? How about the contractor or his crew?"

"Your brothers think we're trying to steal business from Main Street, and Mick accused us of being selfish."

"Mick means well." Misty waved her hand. "He wouldn't sabotage our production, especially since you sunk all that money into it and this is my chance to hit the big time."

"You're going to be doing big time if you don't find the thieves," Gordon said. "By the way, Brad, did you know Misty was driving on the runway when that poor dentist crashed his plane?"

"Why, Gordon, you creep." Misty kicked Gordon's ankle, wishing Westie was around to add an ankle bite. "You're the one who told me to take a shortcut. You said the airport was closed."

"Are you two confessing to multiple crimes?" Brad's head swiveled from Gordon to Misty and back like he was watching a tennis match.

"No, definitely not," Gordon said. "Has that dentist filed a complaint? Is the FAA going to investigate? Because if not, then I say you close the case and go find the throne thieves."

"The dentist is in shock and cannot communicate," Brad said in a slow, deliberate voice as if he were explaining to two-year-olds. "However, I have information that the airplane is not registered to him. He might have taken it as a joy ride. I won't say he stole it yet unless the owner complains about it."

"Who's the owner of the plane?" Gordon asked.

"It's still under investigation," Brad said, suddenly tight-lipped. "I want you two to find out as much as you can about the mysterious dentist. I did an internet search based on the business card you found in Sam's wallet and there is no dentist named Dr. Samuel Finnegan anywhere in San Francisco."

"That's strange," Gordon said. "No one was supposed to fly into Christmas Creek due to the blizzard. Why would a random unknown man who wants to play Santa Claus just happen to drop in? Where is he, by the way?"

"If you two find out anything, let me know," Brad said, closing his unused notebook. "I've got speeding tickets to give out, crooks to catch, porch bandits to trap, and traffic to clear."

"While you're helping old ladies cross the street, I have a business to run." Gordon cracked his knuckles. "Misty, you need to call a temp agency and get me a big, fat Santa."

"He isn't going to fit on that throne." She eyed the toilet and laughed. "But we already have Sam."

She lowered the lid and sat on the top of the toilet. "It's not too bad."

Brad rolled his eyes and swaggered out of the gazebo, parting the workers and deliverymen. He was about to make an exit when a news reporter stuck a mic in his face. A crowd surrounded them, and to make matters worse, the decorating team had already arrived to witness the spectacle.

What now?

A flash caught Misty's eye, and when she looked up, a reporter was taking pictures of her sitting on the toilet with Gordon standing next to her.

"No pictures. No pictures." He held out his hand and blocked the lens. "There's nothing going on here. Get. Get."

Another reporter stuck a mic in Misty's direction. "Can you tell us more about the surprise Santa and his substitute throne?"

"I, uh, no comment," she started, and then decided, why not? "We're going to have a blast here at Christmas Village at Southside Glen. As you can see, fun and games are awaiting you, and our elusive Santa is missing his throne."

She gave a flourish at the American Standard toilet and jiggled the handle. "Have you been naughty this year? Santa's Throne knows all."

Gordon was beside himself, but he knew better than to bluster while cameras were around. Instead, he gritted his teeth in a tight grin resembling a constipated cookie jar thief. When the reporter interviewed him, he managed to say, "You'll have to come back on opening day to see whether our Santa gets his throne back."

"Who is your Santa?" a female reporter asked. "Is he that hunky dentist Miss Jolly introduced at the Christmas carol marathon?"

"We'll have several Santas," Gordon began.

"I thought there was only one Santa Claus in the entire world," the woman whined. "What do you mean many Santas?"

"Rest assured Santa will be by," Misty said. "After all, we have toys and dolls, trains and planes, candy canes and gumdrops, kitty cats and puppy dogs, and everything a child could wish for. Come back Monday. He'll be here!"

The gathered workers and passersby clapped and cheered, pointing to someone behind Misty.

"Woof, woof, woof," Westie yipped, charging onto the gazebo with his red silk cape flying behind him. He leaped onto the toilet lid and howled to the moon, wagging his stubby little tail.

Somehow, in the tumult of reporters trying to interview the terrier, Gordon was able to steer Misty behind a construction fence where Ivy was painting sets and Holly was stapling up tinsel.

"Let me show you how serious this kerfuffle is," Gordon said. "We not only have those pesky reporters out there videoing the mess, but a spy in our midst."

"A spy? What do you mean?"

Gordon shoved his electronic tablet in Misty's face. "Emails from Dastardly Dash. He seems to know about the iced-over flower beds as well as the dentist you proposed to sit in for Santa."

Misty hastily skimmed the emails. "It could be anyone who heard me make that speech last night."

"How about the ice on the flowerbeds and the huge snowdrifts?" He eyed Misty with a suspicious glare.

"Anyone in town could have driven by and seem them. Or the decorators talked. I wouldn't call it spying," Misty said. "Maybe someone uploaded pictures to social media."

"Or maybe you've been whispering in his ear," Gordon said. "I didn't tell anyone but you about my toothache."

"Oh, come on, Holly must know," Misty countered.

"Holly's not the spy," Gordon shot back.

"Did I hear my name?" Holly sauntered over. "What are you picking on my sister about now?"

Ivy tagged along and put down her paintbrush. "Maybe Sam is the spy. I saw him glancing at you when you bit down on a plum pit."

"Who'd leave a pit in the pudding?" Gordon groused. "You're right. It could be Sam. Did Brad tell you the airplane's not registered to Sam?"

"No, he's been too busy investigating," Ivy said. "He really needs to hire a deputy. He can't do everything by himself, especially since you're tripling the town's population for your Christmas Extravaganza Experiences, Episodes One, Two, and Three."

"Where *is* Sam?" Misty cast her eyes around the convention center which was a hive of activity. "Anyway, I need to go through my checklists and make sure everything is on track."

Powering up her tablet, she dashed toward Mrs. Claus's Bed and Breakfast. If *Sam* was the spy trying to sabotage her work, he was going to have to answer to her, shock or no shock.

* * *

Dash was busily typing on Mrs. Claus's computer when she peeked her head into his room.

"Yoohoo, I see a busy little bee buzzing her way over here." Mrs. Claus made a zipping motion over her lips.

"Thanks for calling in the tip about the toilet swap," Dash said. "Did Misty get on TV?"

"She most certainly did. This is going to be great publicity for you. Everyone's going to want to come and see what happens."

Dash closed the laptop and shoved it under the bed. "You are a gem. What would Santa do without you?"

Flirting with Mrs. Claus, otherwise known as Constanza Zingerman, was so easy, but he'd better put a zipper over his lips as the sleigh bells hanging on the bed and breakfast door jingled.

Constanza waddled through the sitting room. "Why, Misty, I just saw you on TV."

"Is Sam here? It's imperative I speak to him." She sounded so serious.

"Why, he's unable to talk, you know that," Con said. "The shock. The utter shock of crashing his plane."

"It's not his airplane," Misty said. "Brad told me it's registered to someone else."

"Oh my, the poor man. He not only crash-landed, but he didn't get into the right plane."

Misty barged into Dash's room, finding him lying on the bed with his hands behind his head.

Dash raised a pair of surprised eyebrows and sat up. He pasted a silly grin on his face and held out his hands for a hug.

"Oh, Sam." Misty fell into his arms. "I'm so glad you're okay. You won't believe what's happened this morning. I got up late because I couldn't sleep last night. Thinking about you and everything we did."

"Oh?" Mrs. Claus, the gossipy kind, didn't miss a beat. "Whatever is wrong? I hope you two didn't get into a fight."

"No, we're good," Misty said. "But Gordon's upset and he showed me some email from Dash Weston."

Dash put a confused look on this face to convey innocence and curiosity.

"I know this probably has nothing to do with you," Misty said. "But Mr. Weston approved your idea for the snowdrifts and the ice pond over the flowerbeds."

"Oh my, that's wonderful, Sam, isn't it?" Constanza's wink was too obvious.

Fortunately, Misty was staring into Dash's eyes as if she could discern whether he was true blue or not. His blues could rival hers, so he kept his gaze on her and made bedroom eyes to boot.

"It is wonderful." Misty picked up Con's lead. "Mr. Weston not only approved your idea about the snow play area, but also said more power to me for having you do the Santa gig for free. Is it true you'll do all nine days?"

Dash nodded and smiled closemouthed, keeping his gaze melting and desirous on Misty's baby blues.

"Ahhh, that's so generous of you," Con provided the commentary.

"There's only one problem," Misty said. "How did Mr. Weston know all these details? Gordon thinks there's a spy in our midst."

"Why would that be a problem?" Con interrupted. "Mr. Weston is the main investor in the Christmas Village concept. He should know how it's going. If you've nothing to hide, why worry about reports going back to him?"

"I'm not worried," Misty said. "But Gordon wonders how Mr. Weston knew he had a toothache."

"Gordon is one big toothache himself." Constanza huffed, putting her hands on her hips. "I know he's a motherless boy and all that, but your sister ought to train him better. Now, you two run along and enjoy the day. And Sam, I thank your generosity for helping us out. Don't worry, we'll treat you well and we do most certainly hope you'll settle in our town. God knows we have a lot of toothaches around here."

Dash gave her a curt salute and a nod, and Con took the liberty to hug him so tight, she almost squeezed the air out of him. Of course, she knew his little secret, that he could speak, so he supposed he had to put up with a bit of extra smothering.

He glanced at Misty and didn't like what he saw. She was scowling at Constanza's back and had one finger on her cheek, and he could see the gears in her mind turning.

Was she onto him?

He'd better be more careful in his future emails to Gordon. He hadn't expected the monster to share it with Misty, but then again, he'd bet Gordon didn't show his defamatory email to Misty, the one where he accused the Sam character of playing to Misty's insecurities.

One thing Dash knew for sure. Misty had nothing to be insecure about.

She was about to get the promotion of her lifetime that would lift her above anyone in this small dinky Christmas town.

Chapter Thirteen

Dash had a wonderful breakfast with Constanza, but unfortunately without Misty. She had a million billion things to do, and after checking that he was okay, as well as his alibi—Constanza had vouched for him—she rushed back to Christmas Village.

"I have to go into town to pick up my friend Ruth," Constanza said. "Would you like a ride? I know you lost all your luggage, and I bet you're not really going to wear the Kris Kringle's little brother outfit your entire stay."

"They're calling me Sam Single," Dash said. "But Gordon is intent on hiring what he calls a real Santa. He thinks I'm too muscular to be Santa."

"You know what I think?" She poked his abs. "You're perfect. Maybe too young and healthy, but you'll draw a crowd. At least for the first session. Everyone will want to see whether you'd sit on that toilet, and you'll be the perfect surprise. However, we need to change it up a bit."

"You mean a different Santa for the second and third session?"

"Yep. And make it a surprise."

"Where am I going to find two Santas who aren't Nick Jolly at such short notice?" Dash asked.

"Didn't know you were in charge." Constanza gave him a sidewise glance.

"I'm not, but I want Misty to be successful. She's got real talent. Did you see how she whipped up the crowd at the caroling marathon? Got everyone curious to come down here."

"I sure did, and I'm proud of her. She might be one of the younger Jolly twins, but she's got Christmas in her blood like all the rest of them." Constanza gave him a nudge. "When are you going to let her know you got your voice back? A man can do a lot more romancing with words."

"And a man can do a lot of loving without words," Dash said. "Do you have anything more inconspicuous in the costume closet for me?"

"You mean bright-blue lederhosen isn't your thing?" Constanza chuckled, and her bosom heaved good-naturedly. "I'm sure I can find something more appropriate for an incognito shopping trip."

"While you're looking, can I borrow your phone? I'll get a new one, but I'll need to make a few calls right away."

Constanza unlocked her cell phone and handed it to Dash. She took the liberties of giving him a kiss on the cheek and a pat on the back before sauntering off with an exaggerated hip swing.

Dash contacted his assistant, Darlene, who was really his sister. "Hey, it's me. If the pesky sheriff is asking around, tell him Sam Finnegan is an employee of Weston International and has my permission to fly that airplane."

"What the heck happened out there?" Darlene's voice was so shrill it fried his ear hairs. "Dad, Mom, Aunt Sharky, and all of Dad's girlfriends, er, mystery shoppers, are worried sick about you."

"I had to make an emergency landing," Dash explained. "They must have closed the airport after I filed my flight plans, and no one bothered to radio me. Tell that sheriff I'm suing the town. The runway wasn't lit. It was covered with snow, and if I hadn't been rescued by that young lady driving her Jeep, I would have frozen to death."

"I heard through the grapevine she was the cause of your crash. Driving on the runway."

"What runway?" Dash shouted. "There were no markings and no lights. Nothing. Maybe an area that was smoother than the rest, but it was covered with snow. Anyway, I'll swear to a court that I couldn't tell where the runway was, so I'm sure she couldn't either. Besides, all traces and tracks were covered with snow. All I saw was the giant snow plow sitting idle and unattended. If they charge either me or the young lady with any crime, Weston International will sue the pants off that town."

"Got it. Got it. Want me to head down and mystery tour?"

"I've got it under control. They believe I'm Dr. Sam Finnegan."

"Not the sheriff," Darlene said. "Gordon put him in contact with me, and I told him you were one of our mystery shoppers, an employee, so he knows you're not a dentist, but he doesn't know you're Dash Weston."

"Keep it that way for now. I hope the sheriff will keep his mouth shut."

"He seems like the tight-lipped kind, always looking for a crime. I wouldn't worry he'd blab. More like he'll try and trap you into confessing."

"I've nothing to confess. You let him know about the FAA violations, or even better, call in the FAA."

"Actually, holding it over their head is better," Darlene, who also got her business sense from their father, suggested. "I'll get on it. Also, I'll activate your Sam Finnegan credit cards, but you be careful out there. The townsfolk might not react well when they find out they've been trolled. I heard they really want a dentist."

"With the amount of sweets and goodies they imbibe and celebrating Christmas year-round, I'd agree. You won't believe it, but I had to suck down a plum pudding the other night to get them to think I'm Sam Single."

"Who's Sam Single?"

"My nickname. Kris Kringle's little brother. I'm the one who pulled the stunt swapping the heated throne with the toilet."

"It's brilliant," Darlene gasped. "Bookings are up sky-high. I think we might be overbooked."

"Great! You handle any calls from Gordon by being mysterious, and I'll call you from my new phone once I get it. Don't call back on this one. It belongs to Constanza Zingerman who's running Mrs. Claus's Bed and Breakfast."

"Okie dokie. Touch base later," his sister said. "And one more thing. What's with that Gordon Gekko calling me a secretary? That's so twentieth century."

"People here are a little more backwards than in S.F. But so far, I like it."

"You have the hots for little Miss Jolly," Darlene teased. "I saw the video from the Christmas caroling. I've never seen you so smitten."

"Grrrr..." Dash growled and hung up.

* * *

Misty had never worked harder her entire life. She ran to and fro on sore feet, checking in with each vendor, merchant, and supplier. She saw to it that the animal adoption center was stocked with food, water, and toys for the pets to be. She supervised the removal of unneeded materials and debris and marked the construction of the fence around the outdoor ice-skating area, as well as the ramps and stairs leading to the top of the snowdrifts. She checked the stock at the concession stands and called the temp agencies to ensure they hired their quota of elves, gingerbread men, fairy princesses, toy soldiers, and other characters who would be helping at the village and entertaining guests. She also verified the cleaning service schedule and wrote the check for private security guards. Every *i* had to be dotted and every *t* had to be crossed.

She didn't even have time to look for *Sam* or catch a breather when one of the character actresses waved at her with a snowflake wand. The woman was wearing a wizard's hat with stars and moons, a white wig braided into two pigtails, and a blue, fur-lined gown studded with crystals, glittery snowflakes, and silver sequins.

"May I help you?" Misty asked. "Are you looking for your booth?"

"I'm the Christmas fortune-teller, Jacklyn Frost. You look like you need your fortune told." The middle-aged woman turned Misty's hand palm up.

"I'm actually really busy right now," Misty said. "I'm the event coordinator for the Christmas Village Extravaganza. Is there something I can get for you?"

"I sense a high anxiety level." Jacklyn patted Misty's hand. "It'll all work out. You'll see."

"Thanks. I appreciate the pep talk," Misty said. "I'll stop by your booth sometime for a reading."

Jacklyn touched Misty's shoulder with the tip of her snowflake wand. "I see romance in the air. Have a magical evening."

With a swish of her silk skirt, the fortune-teller wandered away, shaking glitter from her snowflake wand as she walked.

Misty was glad the casting company had sent her a variety of Christmas characters. She hadn't expected a fortune-teller, but this would be yet another unique feature for the Southside project. As long as Jacklyn said what people wanted to hear, she would add to the festive atmosphere and generate buzz to attract more visitors.

* * *

It was well into the evening before the last workman boxed up his tools and Misty was able to drag her tired feet to Mrs. Claus's Bed and Breakfast where *Sam* had promised to meet her.

He was more than a sight for sore eyes. In fact, he'd had a complete makeover. His goatee was trimmed and his silver hair was smoothed back, but best of all he was wearing clothes that made him look distinguished and cool—a pair of black slacks, a black turtleneck, and a black glove leather jacket. The only accessory he wore, which she approved heartily, was a red-and-green tartan scarf.

"Sam!" She enveloped him in her arms and hugged him. "You got cleaned up."

He cleared his throat, rasping. "Gggr... getting, muh, my vvvoic"—*cough, cough, cough*—"buh back."

"You're talking!" Misty exclaimed. "That means you're getting over your shock. That's wonderful."

He coughed something unintelligible, and she put her hand on his chest. "I bet your vocal cords are tight. Don't strain yourself, but did you have a wonderful day?"

He nodded brightly and pointed to two pairs of ice skates next to his bed.

"You want to go ice-skating? At the swimming hole?"

"Buh, both." He took a swallow of water from a cup.

"Oh, right. Let's be the first to try out the Flowerbed Pond, and then, I'll take you out to the swimming hole if you're up for it."

He nodded, and she cut off any further explanations with a hot, torrid kiss. He returned the kiss ardently, and Misty wouldn't have minded staying in his room a while longer, but Mrs. Claus barged in with a load of towels.

"Oops, I didn't mean to interrupt." She placed the towels and several sheets of paper on the dresser. "Got the information you needed. This is the most updated map of our town. Oh, and Ruthie says Chief Jerry will be glad to take a turn at being Santa, and Kitty's father, who's visiting, wants to do the Kwanzaa Festival."

Sam stiffened and nodded quickly, as if wanting Mrs. Claus to barge out, but knowing Constanza, or Auntie Con as the town called her, was not one to shush up easily.

"Why, Sam, are you trying to pass the Santa buck?" Misty asked. "I thought you agreed to do all three Extravaganza Experience Episodes."

"You can't expect a frisky young man to sit through all nine days on a Santa throne, can you?" Con answered for *Sam*. "I suggested we change it up. Of course, I should have asked you first since you're the event coordinator."

"Yes, you should have. Gordon is railing on me to call around for a more suitable Santa, but Mr. Weston sent him an email agreeing to Sam. I bet the only reason was that Sam wasn't charging."

"Jerry and Kenton aren't charging either," Constanza said. "Ruthie is tickled pink that Jerry gets to be it. You know how it is in this town, too many Santas and not enough elves."

All three of them laughed at Constanza's joke.

"Okay, then, that sounds like a plan. If it's okay with you, Sam."

Sam nodded eagerly and rasped, "Muh, more time wwwiff yoouw."

"Ah, you're so sweet." Misty gave *Sam* a big smacking kiss. "I can't wait to show you around. Looks like you already have a map, but I know places that are not on the map. Wanna hang out with me?"

His grin was wide and sexy, and he stood, holding out his arm for her to take.

Misty half expected Westie to answer with a bark or a yap, but the little dog was nowhere in sight.

"Have you seen Westie lately?" she asked. "He was around earlier while my sisters were decorating and the kids were painting the gingerbread doghouses. Could he be hiding in one of them?"

"Wuh-wuhf-tee?" *Sam* shrugged and made motions like either here or there.

"Oh, shush. Don't worry about Westie," Constanza huffed. "The little darling is making himself at home all across Christmas Creek. I wouldn't be surprised if he raises the most money at the pet adoption auction."

"I guess I shouldn't be selfish and keep him to myself or Sam," Misty said. "But he really does resemble you—silver hair, beard, and all."

"Woof." He took her hand and picked up the skates, throwing them over his broad shoulder, and Misty was glad she had *Sam* all to herself without any nosy, pesky chaperones. Maybe the fortune-teller was right about her romantic future.

Chapter Fourteen

Misty and *Sam* held hands as they skated circles on the frozen Flowerbed Pond. One side of it bordered the concrete wall of the convention center, and the other side was edged with the low walls of the planting area. A few of the local teenagers joined them, and others threw snowballs up and down the piles of snow set aside for lid and basket riding. Misty had made a decision to forego real sleds with their steel runners after checking with the event insurance agent, and the local home goods store agreed to sell laundry baskets and plastic garbage can lids for the activity.

The ice-skating section also had to pass inspection. The construction workers added plexiglass barriers reinforced with metal fence posts to keep people from falling off the raised beds. They hand-groomed the ice, and it was smooth and solid due to the low ambient temperature. Addition piles of snow were moved around the perimeter so that anyone who fell either off the hill or ice would land on something soft.

"This feels so much more real than an artificial rink," Misty said, taking a deep breath of the nippy air underneath a gray sky. "But it still doesn't beat the swimming hole."

"Wuh, why?" *Sam* asked, looking like a curious kid who'd been locked up in an attic all his life.

"The surroundings are important. The ice here is great, I'll admit, but we're looking at walls. It just doesn't have the atmosphere of being out in the countryside." She twirled around and raised her hands to the sky. "Something's always different, whether it's a bush with red berries frosted over or a red cardinal flying overhead. Where a dropped pinecone or a pile of scattered branches tells a story. And then there are the memories. The first time on skates. Learning to swim."

He nodded but she wasn't sure he understood.

She leaned close to him and kissed him. "I'll show you. Ready? Close your eyes, then hold my hands and make a wish."

He did as she told him, smiling faintly and completely trusting her. Skating backwards, she pulled him around in circles—turning around and around, tighter and higher until they were spinning with their arms around each other.

Arms, legs, and skates tangled together and before she knew it, they were flat on their backs, laughing and rolling over each other.

"Memories. See what I mean?" Misty chortled once they were both back on their skates again. "Now, let's race over to the swimming hole before it gets too dark."

"What's wrong with skating in the moonlight?" *Sam* asked, then looked amazed at his words.

"You're speaking complete sentences! Your wish must have come true."

Instead of agreeing, he covered his mouth and nodded, as if he didn't want to talk more.

"Aren't you happy?" Misty asked. "You're no longer in shock."

He stared at her, eyes wide. "I'm cured. Who knew falling down ice-skating would unshock me?"

"I can't wait to tell everyone," Misty said. "Now you can properly ask the children what they want for Christmas and do your proper ho, ho, hos. I'm so excited."

He shook his head so vehemently he resembled a terrier shaking the life out of a rat. "No, please, don't tell. I don't want to ruin my vacation looking inside people's mouths or giving them advice. I just want to experience all there is to Christmas Creek and observe everything."

"I get it." She giggled. "You don't want the suspicious sheriff to question you. That's fine, but you have to tell me if you stole that airplane or not."

"I had permission to use it. It's insured and everything is taken care of. You weren't driving on the runway. In fact, the runway wasn't visible because they forgot to plow the snow."

"Indeed!" Misty exclaimed. "It's a good thing neither one of us died."

"Exactly." He hugged her tightly and shuddered. "Then I'd never have this memory with you."

"Let's go make more, and don't worry, I won't make you talk to anyone else." She smushed his lips with another kiss. Oh, how she loved his kisses. They made her melt and wish for happy endings. "But you have to promise to tell me everything."

"I'll only talk when we're alone. Just warning you. No talking even on the Santa throne. You can say I'm the Silent Santa."

"As long as you put that tongue of yours to good use, I'm not complaining." She tangled her tongue with his in a most luscious kiss.

"Ahem, ahem." A booming voice which could only belong to Bossy Gordon cut in. "This here is a G-rated family venue. If you'll excuse me, Sam, I need a debrief from Miss Jolly."

"Sorry, I've already worked way over time," Misty said. "You'll find all my reports in your email. Sam and I are on a date. Bye!"

She pulled out the Jeep keys Merry handed her when she dropped the vehicle off and headed toward the parking garage arm in arm with her Silent Santa.

* * *

Since most of the roads were cleared, Misty had no trouble taking her Jeep and *Sam* on the secret backroads through Christmas Creek and its surrounding hills and valleys. She drove him from Southside Glen through stands of redwood forests and rolling farmlands. They wound their way by the old sawmill where the timber industry started with Gordon Gills' great-great-grandfather. They crossed the creek through a covered bridge, and of course, she and *Sam* stopped for a kiss inside the Kissing Bridge and then jiggled their way creekside by Holly's cabin which she rented to Kitty, Mick's girlfriend.

Kitty's father, Kenton, was chopping firewood, and they stopped by for a visit. He was looking forward to being Santa for the after-Christmas segment, December 26, 27, and 28. Misty decided rather than reproduce the previous experiences, she would do a huge sale event, as well as combine the celebration with Kwanzaa—letting Kitty and her father drive the events all the way to New Year's Eve.

She gave Kenton and Kitty a budget and the passwords to make it happen, and when she asked *Sam* what he thought, he was agreeable and supportive.

"I'm afraid of Gordon's reaction," Misty said after leaving Kitty's cottage. "Although I know Kitty is a great planner too, and her father is handy with the tools. He's thinking of redecorating the throne once we find it."

"I'll let you in on a secret," *Sam* whispered. "I was walking around in the village after everyone went home, and I might have seen some elves swapping the throne."

"Why, you sneak!" Misty mock-punched him. "Why didn't you stop them?"

He pointed to his throat. "No words. I barked, and they laughed and assured me they were playing a prank on Gordon."

"Ugh. Gordon would blow his kneecap if he knew. Did you recognize the elves? Were they my brothers?"

"My lips are zipped," *Sam* said. "Although this throne swap is turning out to get a lot of media attention. Those pictures have gone viral, and we're going to have a huge turnout of people curious to whether I have to sit on a toilet for three days."

"Oh, wow! I didn't even think of it as a publicity stunt. As long as the elves promise to bring back the heated throne."

"Somehow, I think they will," *Sam* said. "But they made me promise not to tell, and I shouldn't have told you."

"Of course you should share with me. It's my head on the line. If this stunt blows up, I'll never get to plan even a children's playdate, much less events for princes, presidents, and billionaires."

He tickled her under her chin and lifted her face. "I've a feeling you will be so famous and sought after, you won't remember to return my phone calls."

"You're just saying it to be sweet, but I'll remember to always return your calls." She ended her stalwart statement with a kiss on his lips. "I'm really starting to like you, Sam I Am."

"I've liked you the moment you pulled me out of that wreckage," he said between kisses. "You seemed like an angel."

"Oh, then you don't know how I really am. A category five hurricane." She pulled out of his kisses and dragged him by the arm. "Let's go skinny-dipping in the swimming hole."

"Kidding?" he yelped.

"Skinny-skating then," she laughed at his bulging eyes popping out of his head.

Driving at a breakneck speed, Misty zoomed up Gill Road and passed Gills Mansion, then hung a wild turn where the old carriage house and stables had fallen into ruins. She traced her way through a dark and abandoned road, past spooky low-hanging trees. Once the poorly marked road ended, Misty off-roaded the Jeep between snow-covered bushes and shrubs down into a hollow of land with a solidly frozen pond in the center. A weathered sign hung half off its post, and the split-rail fence surrounding the pond was broken in several places.

"Isn't this private property?" *Sam* asked.

"Technically, but the moonshiners used to hang out here," Misty said. "And I'm not sure whoever has this claim remembers it. There's a system of caves where they used to hide their kegs and the remnants of an old still around here and the best sledding down Moonshine Alley."

"None of this is on the map Auntie Con gave me," *Sam* said. "What other secrets do you keep?"

"I'll tell you only if you go skinny-skating with me." She parked the Jeep beside a knoll of snowy shrubs laced with ice crystals. "Come on, chicken, what are you waiting for?"

"I don't believe you're going to skinny-skate," he taunted her. "You'll freeze your tushie off!"

"I dare you!" She climbed into the back of the Jeep and took off her boots. "I'm not showing you any more of Christmas Creek unless you join me in the middle of the swimming hole."

"It's frozen solid."

Wiggling her behind, she lowered her wool pants. "Lucky us, because we won't be going skinny-dipping, unless the ice breaks."

"We'll die!" he exclaimed, except his teeth gleamed with a sneaky smile.

Misty made a vow to herself. If *Sam* took the dare, then he would be crazy enough to keep up with her. If not, then it was better to know now before she fell in love with him. So far, none of the guys she'd slowed down enough to date had taken her up on her dares.

Her thighs felt the bite of cold, but she stripped off her pants and laced up her skates. She left her panties on, and she wasn't going to ask *Sam* to remove his boxers. She wasn't a sadist, but she had to see how far he'd go.

Watching him out of the corner of her eye, she unwound her scarf and tossed her hat and earmuffs. She could only afford a few minutes before frostbite set in, so she had to make it quick.

Her breath hissed from her numb lips as she unzipped her parka, sloughed it off her shoulders, and then in one crazy tug, she yanked her sweater over her head and threw her clothes on the tailgate of the Jeep.

"Woohoo! Race you!" Her teeth chattered, and prickles of ice pierced every piece of exposed skin. Head down, she skated with all her might over the frozen swimming hole. Everything stung, from the top of her scalp to the tips of her fingers as she twirled and made toe loops over the ice.

Hurry, hurry, hurry, she begged under her breath, not sure how long she could keep up the skinny-skating to give *Sam* a chance to unlock her heart.

A skidding sound and a spray of ice hit her face. Frozen fingers locked on to hers. She blinked ice from her eyelashes and a smile cracked her face. *Sam* was bare-chested, bare-legged, and wearing only his tighty-whities.

"You're a brief guy and not a boxer man," she yelped.

"I'm too cool for boxers. Now, am I man enough for you?" He winked, although it looked like his eyelashes froze together for a second.

"Yes!" She flung her arms around him, stealing as much warmth as she could from him, and together, they circled the pond, hand in hand, but not as smoothly as they'd skated at the Flowerbed Pond.

Oh no. She was so frozen, she didn't know if she'd ever thaw out.

"Enough?" *Sam* asked after they completed a hurried and rushed circle.

"Yeh, yeh, yeh." Her teeth juddered so hard, she couldn't even kiss him properly, and he had to practically drag her frozen, stiff limbs back to the Jeep.

Thank God she'd left the engine running and the heat turned up full blast. She tumbled into the back and scrambled with her clothes, unable to get her skates off.

He dressed her first, pulling the sweater down over her head, and wrapping her with her parka. His skin was ice-cold as she helped him replace his black turtleneck, pants, and that soft glove-leather jacket she so wanted to snuggle with.

They were down to unlacing the skates when he found a pack of chemical hand warmers she'd forgotten about. He activated the warmers, as many as he could, and somehow, between the heater and the warmers, and her blood regaining circulation, she retied her boot laces and roped him around the neck with his red-and-green tartan scarf, wrapping him up with a bow.

Their faces met square on, cold lips touching and then warming up with a hot kiss.

"Now that makes skinny-skating all worth it," he murmured into the kiss.

"Yes, and now you deserve to be let into a secret." She pulled his black watch cap down to cover his ears. "I promised."

"It's not on the map?"

She shook her head. "I never shared it with anyone. It's too dangerous."

"Nothing scares me more than your dares." He rubbed his hands together and stuffed chemical warming packs into his gloves. "But you did promise, so let's get to it."

"Okay, here we go, but you have to close your eyes while I drive."

"Why? You don't want me to find it again?"

"Partly, but it'll be too scary with your eyes wide open." She tapped him. "Now, cover those eyes. I'll know if you're peeking when I hear you scream."

Misty put the Jeep in gear and zigzagged up a narrow set of switchbacks. It was hard to see in the dark, and she had to be careful not to drive off a cliff. No one, not even her parents, knew about this secret place. They would chastise her greatly, and if she encouraged others to try and find the place, someone could get hurt.

She idled the Jeep, creeping as close to the edge of the overhang as she could, then set the parking brake and transmission.

"Okay, you've been a good boy and you didn't peek." She leaned over and took *Sam's* hands from his face.

His eyes grew so big and round, they matched the full moon above as he beheld the colorful lights of the town below them.

"It looks like a snow globe diorama. A Christmas wonderland."

She snuggled close and held his hand. "That's Christmas Creek in a nutshell."

"You can see everything for miles." He pointed north. "Isn't that the airport? It looks like the lights are on."

She looked up at the moon. "There's a plane with landing lights, and look, up there."

"I can almost see Santa's sleigh, and is that the mansion?" He craned his neck at the towers that were so lit they looked like they were covered with crystals.

"Yes, Gordon has a huge electric bill ever since he became Holly's boyfriend. That's where the Gala Ball is held on Christmas Eve."

"I'm signed up for the one at Southside Glen," he said. "But I wonder what the real one is like. How will I know if the one at the convention center is like the real one?"

"You have to come with me to the real one," Misty said. "Lucky that Jerry will be Santa on the second Extravaganza Experience Episode."

"Yes. Lucky me. Now that you mention it, I really did overcommit to being Sam Single all nine days. I'm glad you pared it down to three days pre-Christmas because it gives me a chance to experience the rest of it with you."

"I feel the same about you." She rested her head against his strong shoulders. "I'm glad you dropped in on us."

"Me too." He held her close, and Misty's heart leaped off the overlook, flying high above her town and safe in the arms of her soul mate, *Sam*.

"I named this place Heart's Leap," she said. "Whenever I'm sad or disappointed or my heart is broken, I come here and take a leap of faith."

"You're not sad or disappointed right now, are you?"

"Oh, no, because you're the only soul I've ever brought here, and I'll leap if you leap."

"Our hearts will leap together." He clasped her hands in both of his. "Ready? Wheee!"

Their lips joined and their souls knit in a dizzying kiss as shooting stars flared above and the lights of Christmas sparkled in a panoramic view below.

* * *

Dash had never met a woman as open and honest about her feelings as Misty Jolly. She didn't play games and hold back her opinions. She simply told him she liked him and wanted to take a leap of faith with him. His heart had joined hers in the leap, but he had to be careful and guard it well. His mother had not married well, and his Aunt Sharky was still single and very picky.

"What are you thinking about?" Misty asked as they drove down the forested hillside toward the twinkling town lights below.

"How enchanting these forests are," he said. "The sparkling ice crystals on the trees and the fresh snow, so clean and pure. I'm not sure it's possible to recreate this winter wonderland indoors at Southside Glen."

"Oh, Sam, it's so sweet of you to worry about Southside Glen, but thanks to your idea of using the snowdrifts outside, the kids will still get a smidgen of a taste of the great outdoors."

"Flowerbed Pond doesn't match up to all of this." He swept his hand over the windshield. "I'm glad you brought me out here."

"Flowerbed Pond has its charm." She sounded like she was teasing. "You and I were the gold-medal ice-skating champs out there."

"Flat on our backs." He laughed heartily. "I'm usually not so klutzy on skates."

"You're a good guy, Sam Finnegan." She pinched his cheek. "Tomorrow's the last day before the opening, and I've still got a ton of things to do."

"You're going to be fine, and if you want, hand me half your list and I'll make sure they get done," he offered.

"I couldn't do that to you. You're a paying guest."

"How do you know I paid?" He waggled his eyebrows. "Maybe I'm your guardian angel dropped in from the sky."

"You know what?" She tilted her chin and winked. "I'm betting you are. Things have gotten a lot better since I met you. Gordon doesn't yell at me as much. Mrs. Claus is happier by a mile, and then there's that sweet little Westie who's staying with Dr. Dale and Dottie. I sure hope he's not getting into any trouble."

"I'm sure he's fine. Who knows, maybe he's found a home, too."

"Like you have?" Her expression was hopeful, a little too much so, and it churned his gut because the town could use a dentist, and he wanted to explore this thing with Misty, but how, how, how could he stay on? Mystery shoppers had to remain a mystery.

"I'll help you tomorrow. With everything," he promised.

"That's sweet of you, but why? What's in it for you?"

Good question, he thought. What would she think of him if she discovered his ruse?

How exactly could he reveal himself now or ever? He was stuck in a real quandary. He was mystery shopping, and everyone in Christmas Creek knew him as Sam Finnegan. People took pictures with him, and Misty's entire family met him, not to mention the sheriff, the doctor, and Gordon Gills, his partner. Usually, he did his mystery shopping and disappeared. No one would have remembered him, and no one could connect him to Weston International.

"Because it's fun, and I like you," Dash said. "When you become a big star event promoter, I hope you'll look back and remember me and my small role in helping you get started."

She turned the Jeep toward Southside Glen, and his heart dropped because the evening was ending and she wasn't inviting him back to her place.

"You sound like you'll be leaving after Christmas." The corners of her mouth turned down. "But of course you are. You came for a visit, and you have a practice back in the city."

"I can always come back every year," he said, not liking her disappointment.

"Yes, you can." She straightened her shoulders and gave him a stiff smile. "I'm glad I showed you around and gave you some extra experiences."

"I'd like to show you around too," he said. "Invite you to San Francisco for a New Year's Eve celebration."

"That sounds divine."

"Hey, I want to make every night divine for you." He didn't want the night to end.

"It won't be tonight. I have a long day ahead of me." She turned onto the road leading to the convention center. "Not sure I'll get much sleep. There's so much left to do and only one more day to do it all."

"It'll all come together. Don't worry." He put his hand on her shoulder. "I'll help. In fact, I'll make sure of it."

She turned a quizzical expression at him, and he had to remember she didn't know he was Dash Weston.

"You can help as long as it's fun, but it's going to be twenty-four seven until the grand opening. I'll understand if you want to bow out. Everything has to be perfect or Mr. Weston will pull the rest of his investment and leave the entire town in debt. Gordon will be crushed, and the town will have to cut services and raise taxes."

"I didn't know the town was so exposed," Dash said. "I thought you told me Gordon was the main investor."

"I don't remember telling you, Sam Finnegan." She playfully pinched his arm. "That's confidential business, and I don't have loose lips."

"Oh, well then, I must have heard the workmen talking." He leaned over and kissed her lightly. "Misty, I'll do everything I can to make Southside a big success. Winter, spring, summer, and fall. Trust me."

Chapter Fifteen

Dash woke early the next morning, eager to block and tackle any problems Misty might have with the Christmas Village project.

He called Darlene. "Did Dad get my progress report?"

"He did, and he's worried," Darlene said.

"Why? I gave a positive report. Everything's going well. Ticket sales are through the roof, and we're well stocked with food, merchandise, and animals. The cast has been assembled and have rehearsal today. Security is in place. The cleaning and maintenance crews have their assigned slots. The decorations and sets look fantastic, and the Santa Gazebo and Petting Zoo are ready to roll. The missing throne mystery is going viral on social media, and everyone is waiting to see the Santa reveal."

"True, but you know how Dad is. Worried."

"Will he and Zenaya be coming to the grand opening?" he asked about his father and his latest arm candy.

"Incognito. Yes, along with Aunt Sharky. I'll be arriving tomorrow."

"You? Why? Everything is going well."

"Dad's not stupid," Darlene said. "With all the praise you're heaping on Misty Jolly and the pictures of you two gallivanting around town, he's worried you're not objective."

"Misty is doing a great job. You'll see. As for gallivanting around town, I'm getting ideas on improvements for other Christmas Villages around the world."

"Well, okay, but I'm afraid you're in a bit of a pickle," his sister said in that all-knowing voice of hers. "You're being dubbed The Silent Santa due to the way you dropped out of the sky. How are you going to ho, ho, ho and ask the children what they want? Also, we've milked the toilet bowl long enough. I believe we should replace the throne and have a real Santa."

"I promised Misty I'd do the first three days."

"That's exactly the problem. You promised her, but she's not in charge. She's supposed to do what we want and please us, not the other way around. You act like you're in puppy love with her. Are you?"

His sister's directness caught his heart in his throat. Of course, he was fond of Misty, and she was everything he didn't dare hope for. But he couldn't get too attached since he had to disappear or go back to his real identity.

"I don't know how to transition back to Dash Weston," he muttered the problem foremost on his mind. "I definitely don't want to be Silent Sam and go around miming to her family. When she finds out I've been mystery shopping, she's going to want to have nothing to do with me."

"When she finds out you've paid for some of the cost overruns to make her look good, she's really going to explode," Darlene said.

"Why would she be upset if we make her look good?" Dash scratched his head.

"Because it's condescending. Like letting a child win a game," Darlene said. "It's like you believe she's incompetent."

"Oh no, not at all. Misty is awesome. She challenges everyone, from that money-grubbing contractor to that prima donna romance author to the uppity hunks who want custom backgrounds for their stations. She enables them to get their work done, but she doesn't assume anything about anyone. She even allowed the mahjong club to decorate their kiosk without imposing her ideas on them, and the international food court and game section is exactly the way the vendors want to portray."

"Sounds like she's great. If it's any consolation, you're safe for now. She won't blame Sam Finnegan for any of this. You're still the dashing dentist in her mind."

"I can't stay Sam Finnegan forever," Dash said. "Especially since Gordon and Misty are expecting Mr. Weston, me, to show up for the grand opening. Oh great. I'm supposed to cut the ribbon."

"You just now remembered?"

"I hit my head in the plane crash. I had a shock," Dash said. "Is it possible for you to hire an actor to be me?"

"Are you off your rocker?" Darlene yelped. "It'll be better to disappear Sam Finnegan. Then you dye your hair. Put on colored contact lenses and help Misty pick up the pieces of her broken heart."

"Don't you think she'll suspect?"

"Of course she will. But it'll be up to you to let her in on the secret and charm her into keeping the secret for you."

"Then I better do everything I can to make her happy while I still can," Dash said. "Send flowers in Dash's name to Mrs. Claus's Bed and Breakfast for Misty. Write on the card that I heard how hard she's been working and am impressed with her ideas."

"That's a good first step. Anything else?"

"Call the movers and move the Christmas throne to Chance Martin's furniture store during the night. Have them discover it the next day and bring it to Christmas Village. Cover it with a drop cloth, and then when I appear at the gazebo, we'll hold everyone in suspense."

"Good idea. You do the throne reveal, and I'll figure out a way to make the switcheroo. Can't tell you how I'm going to do it so you can make it look real."

"You're so devious, Darlene."

"The rest is up to you, Dash."

"Book me dinner for two at the exclusive Mill Inn. That's how confident I am."

She snickered. "You always double down instead of admitting you're wrong. Ciao!"

* * *

Misty couldn't help being mystified by *Sam's* interest in Southside Glen, but then again, she needed all the help she could get. All night long, Gordon texted her and called her. She had to silence her phone, but it was hard to sleep, knowing all the work still to be done.

Gordon: *Where the heck are you? The bakery truck was delayed due to weather and the loading dock is locked. Get over there right away and call me. There will be a standing-around fee.*

Gordon: *Nate reported a leak around the skylight. Need you to assess and call the water damage cleanup.*

Gordon: *How is the replacement throne coming along? I want the exact upholstery of the original one. Insurance isn't going to cover the inflated amount Chance is charging for a rush job.*

And on and on and on.

At least Mr. Weston sent an email to Gordon, copying her with how pleased he was with the Santa's Throne Mystery and the publicity they got.

Misty replied with her recommendations. She also rushed to the loading dock and opened the doors wide, thanked the delivery driver, and accepted his invoice along with the extra fee. She called the furniture maker, negotiated him down twenty percent, and promised Chance an extra batch of her mother's famous pecan logs for the trouble. Considering Chance's wife just had a baby, she was grateful he was willing to put in the extra hours.

Ivy promised to locate the upholstery in her decorator's warehouse, and Holly said she could fix up a set of blowup reindeer and snowmen to sit on top of the water-damaged floorboards.

After a hasty breakfast, she found *Sam* raking hay in the petting zoo. "That's sweet of you, but I don't want to put you to work."

"There's still so much to do," *Sam* said. "I love animals, and they're bringing in the puppies and kittens. I can take their pictures and catalog them for the adoption event."

Misty gave him a quick kiss and hugged him. "You'll understand if you don't see me much today? I can't entertain you much, but if you're a good boy, I promise you goodies in your stocking Christmas morn."

"Then I'll be sure to wear an extra-long stocking." He grinned into her kiss.

"Don't be naughty." She tapped him and disengaged. "On second thought, be yourself. I like you just the way you are."

And she did. Taking out her phone, she stretched her arm out for a selfie with him so she could remember him the way he was, a Christmas-loving man who'd unselfishly spent his vacation helping the busiest woman in town.

He zipped his lips when he spotted a worker passing by. He was still putting on the #SilentSam act for the big reveal at the grand opening when he promised her he'd find his throne and his voice to surprise the visitors with a hearty ho, ho, ho.

"You're so devious," she whispered. "But I love it. Won't they be surprised when you can talk after all."

Chapter Sixteen

Misty bit what was left of her fingernails as she went over her clipboard and checklist. It was the morning of the grand opening, and she'd been working nonstop from the time she ate dinner at Mrs. Claus's while catching only a few winks of sleep on a cot in a closet.

Sam, the darling man, had kept his word on helping her. He'd lifted boxes. Mopped up messes. Herded goats. Pitched hay and straw and took pictures of all of the puppies and kittens for adoption.

"I can't believe we found the Santa throne at Chance Martin's," Constanza said in a gossipy tone as she washed the breakfast dishes. "You know that boy has a record? Spent years in prison."

"Someone must have dumped the throne at his place as a prank," Misty said, finishing her cup of strong coffee. "Why would he steal a throne when he has a newborn baby in the house?"

"You never know. He might have wanted the extra money for the replacement. Was there a ransom note?"

"Obviously, no." Misty shook her head and patted Mrs. Claus. "We believe in redemption and forgiveness here."

"Are you going to pay for the replacement he was working on? I know Gordon's worried about cost overruns." Constanza lowered her voice. "I don't want to pry, but are we going to be profitable? I'm so worried about the town's finances on the line."

"We're going to have a great turnout, and don't tell anyone, but we have a mystery benefactor. Someone's been putting money into our account. Direct deposit."

"Oh, my stars. A guardian angel." Constanza clapped her hand over her bosom. "There is a Santa Claus after all."

"Yes, Constanza, I do believe there is." She smiled as her eyes scanned down the list. "If all goes as expected, I do believe we're going to be raining dollars and close out the year well in the black."

"You go, girl!" Constanza raised her hand, and they exchanged a high five.

The jingle bells clanged over the entrance door.

"My stars." Constanza rushed to the door. "The visitors are coming to check in."

"Sorry to disappoint." Misty recognized her brother, Mick's voice. "But I have a special delivery for a Miss Misty Jolly."

"Oh my!" Misty exclaimed as she almost ran into a large Christmas-themed vase filled with red roses, white lilies, holly berries, and evergreen sprigs. "Is this from Mom and Dad?"

He set the elaborate stand of flowers on the entrance hall table. "Why don't you read the card?"

Misty didn't dare believe they were from *Sam*. After all, he'd been so busy the entire day of preparation and couldn't possibly have slipped away to order flowers. He was still acting as if he couldn't speak, and social media was trending with hashtags #SilentSanta and #SamSingle with wild speculations about whether Santa could get his voice back.

Her fingers trembled as she unfolded the note and read:

My dearest Misty, I have heard great things about you and am exceedingly pleased with all the hard work and ingenuity you put into the Christmas Village project. Your work has convinced me that this type of themed-park shopping experience can be expanded worldwide to incorporate other themes and holidays. I'm deeply impressed with you and would like to invite you to San Francisco on New Year's Eve to explore future opportunities as part of the Weston International team. Will you accept my humble request for your company at the Baytop Lounge, at the top of Reed Tower? A car will be sent for you, and I look forward to discussing business with you to ring in the new year.

Signed, your admirer, Dash Weston

"Oh, my stars!" Constanza hooted. "This is incredible. Mr. Weston sounds pleased as punch."

"Isn't it a bit premature?" Misty turned over the letter to see if there was an addendum. "We haven't succeeded yet."

"Oh, but he's a businessman and he has projections. I'm sure he ran the numbers," Constanza said.

"Looks like you have two secret admirers," Mick teased. "Silent Sam and Dash Weston."

"Sam's not secret," Constanza said. "That man is absolutely head over heels. He's spending his vacation helping Misty instead of touring the town. I saw him get up early this morning to practice his Santa schtick. Although I'm not sure about the sign language, but then, he'll be a good listener for sure."

"I'm not sure I should accept this invitation," Misty said. "I can meet Mr. Weston at his office. This New Year's Eve party is too much like a date."

"He says it's business," Mick pointed out. "If you want, Kitty and I can tag along and make sure he keeps his hands off you."

"It's not that." Misty's stomach churned, and she bit the last remaining fingernail. "It's Sam. He's asked me to visit him in San Francisco to ring in the new year, too."

* * *

Misty's head spun at the crowds of happy celebrants trampling through Christmas Village. Everywhere she turned, people were smiling, laughing, taking selfies, and marveling at the replica of Gills Mansion, the Christmas tree under the dome, and buying gifts, food, and toys at the shops and booths. The reenactments of town activities were humming like clockwork.

Romance author, Ebony Cruse, had set up her table full of Christmas romances, and her hunks were dressed like exotic dancing Santas—not at all appropriate to sit on the Santa throne and ask kids their Christmas wishes.

Meanwhile, Craig Brockman and Nutmeg Brown were back with their display of stained glass art and forged horseshoe trivets, door hangers, and wine bottle holders. Misty had heard strange tales about Nutmeg being caught between a Nutcracker soldier and a Rat King at the last Gala Ball, but somehow, she ended up with Craig, a wounded veteran with a prosthetic leg.

Nothing weird or mysterious would happen here at Southside Glen. It was much too modern, electronic, and the schedules ran like clockwork with each activity, encounter, and show timed to the last second.

Misty waved to the people she knew, but she kept her eyes peeled for *Sam*, who'd skipped breakfast at the B&B. The grand opening ceremony was set to start, and Gordon was texting her like crazy.

Sound check right now. Camera crew on hand for Santa's reveal. Mr. Weston has arrived. Meet the limo at the red carpet. Bring scissors. Loose dog running around the food court. Call dogcatcher. Did you hire the fat Santa? We need him to unveil the throne. Go to Mrs. Claus's and get dressed. We need a Mrs. Claus for the Santa reveal. Thermostat too high. Call the coat-check room and order more hangers and tags. Mr. Weston just called. Where are you?

Misty heaved an aggravated groan and silenced her phone. How could she possibly be all those places at the same time. She zigged and zagged like a running back down the football field toward Constanza's place. Gordon could meet Mr. Weston, but she had to support *Sam*. From the looks of it, this was his first Santa gig, and he could be getting cold feet.

"Woof, woof, whirr, ruff, wow." A happy Westie pranced around, bumping against Misty's knees when she jogged through Mrs. Claus's doorway.

"Westie!" She picked him up. "You're good luck, and you're back. Con, I need to dress up as Mrs. Claus for Sam. Where's Sam, by the way? The throne reveal is in five minutes. Mr. Weston's at the gate."

"Slow down, child," Constanza said. "I've got your sexy Santa miniskirt laid out already. You just have to strip and step into it. Gordon already alerted me."

"Oh, good. Did you see Sam?"

"No, but I'm sure he's on his way to the gazebo. He knows he's the star of the show. Don't you be fretting."

"I'm trying to stay calm." She flung her way into the room she was staying in. The red outfit with the white fur trim was shorter than she expected, but with the red fishnet stockings, she was adequately covered. After reapplying her red lipstick and fitting the Santa's hat over her mess of curly hair, she picked up Westie and made her way through the throngs of celebrants to Santa's Gazebo.

"Woof, ruff, grrr, woof," Westie barked happily, his stubby tail wagging at all the people.

"There you are," Gordon said. "I thought I told you to meet Mr. Weston at the gate."

"Where's Sam?" Misty asked. "He's supposed to unveil the throne."

"Mr. Weston is supposed to cut the ribbon. Go find him, and we'll deal with your missing Santa man later." Gordon redirected Misty toward the convention center's entrance.

Still carrying a wiggling Westie, Misty ran out the door and slipped on the red carpet. Her arms flailed and Westie went flying. The carpet snagged her heel and pulled off one red glittery pump.

She tumbled backward right into the arms of a man wearing a gray suit.

"Are you looking for me?" he asked in a voice that sounded like *Sam's*. "I'm Dash Weston."

"Yes, Gordon says we're ready for the ribbon cutting." She put her foot back into the errant pump, righted herself, and got a glimpse of the man's face. He was wearing dark sunglasses and was clean shaven. His hair was dark brown, and his teeth gleamed white and straight. It was definitely not *Sam* who was kind of scruffy and awkward.

Misty was so exhausted she figured she was hallucinating, so worried and thinking about *Sam,* that she saw or heard him everywhere.

"Very well," Mr. Weston said. "Lead the way. I like the way everything looks. We're drawing a large crowd. Can't wait to see Santa."

"Uh, yes, me too," she said without conviction. "Let's cut the ribbon first."

Mr. Weston offered her his arm, so she took it. They walked up the red carpet together and stopped to take pictures in front of the sponsor screen. He looked up, still wearing sunglasses, and she spotted the mistletoe.

"Kiss, kiss, kiss," the crowd chanted.

"No, I can't. I'm sorry." She thought about *Sam* and how hurt he would be if she kissed Mr. Weston.

"We're acting for the cameras," Mr. Weston said. "A small one is okay?"

"I guess," she said. "Merry Christmas, Mr. Weston."

"Call me Dash." He bussed her a quickie on her lips, barely touching her. A slice of panic shot through her at both the zing that shouldn't be there and the flashes from nearby cameras recording the event.

"Do you like the outdoor play area?" she asked, just to be saying something.

"It's absolutely brilliant. I heard it was your idea," Dash said. "I want to commend you on the cost cutting."

"Thanks, but it was actually Sam's idea. We had an early visitor who was so excited to come that he accidentally booked a stay before, oh, maybe I shouldn't say, but he's been wonderful, helping me with all the details."

"An early visitor? How did he get a reservation?" Dash asked. "Our website is set up only to sell blocks of dates starting today."

"He must have somehow gotten through, but it's not a problem, is it?" Misty was sweating bullets, hoping she wasn't getting *Sam* in trouble. "He's a real Christmas lover, and he's not charging us for his advice or anything he's doing."

"Then I'd like to meet this Sam. You must introduce us," Dash said smoothly, and again, Misty wondered at how alike they sounded.

She nodded while her stomach churned. Constanza hadn't seen *Sam,* and she just realized she'd lost Westie when she slipped on the red carpet. Oh well, he was well able to take care of himself. She crossed her fingers as she and Mr. Weston stepped onto the event stage where the podium was set up and a giant red ribbon emblazoned with the words "Christmas Village at Southside Glen" hung between two candy cane posts.

Once on stage, Gordon greeted Mr. Weston, and made signs at Misty to go to Santa's throne. He mouthed, "Santa's missing."

Misty nodded and mouthed, "On it."

She scanned the crowd, looking from face to face, and running around clumps of people, but there was no sign of *Sam*. In desperation, she called Constanza.

"Has Sam gone back? I can't find him. I've also lost Westie."

"Sam will be there," Constanza said. "Don't you worry. He said he was your guardian angel. I bet he's busy guarding you, and he'll drop in right when you need him."

"I'm almost to Santa's Gazebo, and there are people gathered around waiting for the reveal. If he's going to drop in, he'd better do it soon. Mr. Weston and Gordon are making speeches, and then they'll head over with the camera crew."

"Take a deep breath. Have some faith. That man won't let you down."

* * *

"I thought I was giving my speech first," Gordon said to Dash as they approached the podium.

"My assistant changed the order," Dash said. "I'll give a short welcome address, cut the ribbon, and then you can go ahead and take credit. I wonder why you told Miss Jolly to leave. She should get some of the credit, too."

"She's the event planner, and she's still on the job," Gordon said, looking unhappy not to go first.

Dash cleared his throat and approached the podium. He lowered his sunglasses and scanned the gathered crowd. He easily spotted his father, sister, and aunt, all incognito and dressed as tourists sporting big cameras, hats, and wearing ugly Christmas sweaters. Next to them, Misty's parents and family, along with many of the townspeople he'd met as *Sam* were cheering and clapping. Most of them were dressed in costumes and played roles welcoming visitors. They hadn't considered Christmas Village to take business away from the town square and had been generous with selling supplies and helping with the delivery and transportation of the visitors to Southside Glen.

There was one woman hovering around the edge who worried him. She was wearing a pointy wizard's hat, a flowing sky-blue gown with snowflakes, crystals, and tinsel interwoven among the satiny ribbons, and she wore a bright-white wig and heavy makeup that disguised her features. She'd given him the creepiest stare when she bumped shoulders with him on the way to the ribbon cutting.

There was something familiar about her, but he was probably imagining things.

His mother hated these shindigs and preferred to spend Christmas in private, far from the maddening crowds. Besides, she was so vain she would never wear a white powdered wig to cover the lush auburn tresses that she was so proud of.

Clearing his throat, he forced his gaze away from the wizard woman. He was in control today. This entire enterprise belonged to him. Aunt Sharky gave him a thumbs-up and his father jerked his head in a "get the game rolling" gesture.

The big moment was here.

"I'm Dash Weston, president and CEO of Weston International," he said. "And I'd like to welcome each and every one of you to Weston International's inaugural Christmas Village at Southside Glen. You are going to have the time of your life as we recreate a delightful Christmas experience for you. I'd like to acknowledge the town of Christmas Creek for their earnest support, and especially your town leader, Gordon Gills, for his generous investment and hard work to make this Christmas Extravaganza Experience possible. It has come to my attention that your town is gifted with an extraordinary event planner, Miss Misty Jolly, who worked night and day to put all of this together for you. Let's put our hands together and give Gordon and Misty a well-deserved round of applause, and then I'll cut the ribbon to let the festivities and fun begin."

Amidst thunderous applause, Dash posed for the ribbon cutting, slapped Gordon's back in congratulations, and stepped down into the crowd. While Gordon made his speech, Dash slipped into a replica of a North Pole phone booth, all red and white striped and festooned with holly and ivy. In a few minutes, he emerged in his red-and-white-striped sweater and his light-blue lederhosen overall shorts. He wore a pair of round horn-rimmed glasses, a white wig, and pasted on his silvery goatee. He stuffed his wool suit, hat, shoes, and accessories into a green-and-red patchwork Santa's bag and sauntered toward Santa's Gazebo.

"Sam! Sam!" Misty's voice greeted him. "There you are. I was so worried you'd forgotten."

"I promised not to let you down," he whispered, kissing her quickly on the lips to disguise his ability to speak. "How do I look?"

She put her hands on her hips and tilted her face, assessing him.

"Your whiskers feel a little weird, and your hair is longer, but I'm so dead tired, I'm probably not seeing straight."

"When was the last time you got a good night's sleep?" he asked.

She yawned, hardly able to cover her mouth. "I'm not going to be able to sleep until New Year's. Are we still going to meet in San Francisco?"

"Does that mean we have a date?"

She nodded. "I'd love to see where you live and where you have your practice."

"Great, then let's meet at the Top of Reed Tower on New Year's Eve."

Her eyes widened a second, but she nodded and smiled. "Yes, that'll do. I've missed you, Sam Finnegan."

"We were together every day since I dropped out of the sky. How could you miss me?"

"You're right. The rest of this week will be hectic, so I'm pre-missing you." She shook her head and waved her hand. "I'm just so confused. Did you see me and Mr. Weston on the red carpet?"

"No, I must have missed the ribbon cutting," he said. "I bet you were doing a great job."

"I was, but if you see any pictures, I don't want you to be concerned. They told me to pose with him under the mistletoe."

"Oh..." Dash swallowed and lowered his gaze away from Misty. "I'd better get set up with the throne reveal. You know we got it back from Chance Martin, right?"

"Yes, yes, no surprises there." She patted his shoulder. "I'd better go and make sure the video crew is ready."

He stayed in the gazebo and watched her give directions, glad that Gordon's speech was so long winded. Hopefully, his father, sister, and aunt hadn't noticed his disappearance and reappearance from the phone booth. He rescanned the crowd and noticed the weird lady staring straight at him. Why was she waving that silly snowflake wand at him?

His heart thundering, he watched the multitude approached the throne.

Gordon got to the gazebo first and collared Misty. "Where the heck is Mr. Weston? We can't have him missing the Santa reveal. But then again, it looks like you haven't replaced that Sam guy so maybe it's for the better."

"What do you mean? Sam's going to be a great Santa. He's friendly and the kids will love him."

"He. Can't. Speak." Gordon glowered. "I thought I told you to replace him."

"Well, you're stuck with him now." Misty stomped her foot, and a cameraman got into their faces.

Immediately, Gordon pasted on a cheesy grin and said, "We have the perfect Santa for the kids, and it's trending on social media. Everyone's talking about Sam Single and how unique he is. Christmas Village is the place to be."

Misty shrugged away from Gordon and came to Dash's side. "Since I'm your Mrs. Claus, or Mrs. Single, can I have a kiss?"

"Gladly," Dash lip-synced, and they kissed for the cameras, long and sweet.

Misty melted in his arms, and she didn't back off until Gordon tapped them out. "That's enough. It's showtime."

"I hope you'll always remember me in this moment. No matter what happens," he whispered in her ear as they turned to the crowd and waved while "Here Comes Santa Claus" played on the sound system.

"You'll do well, Sam," Misty said, all misty-eyed at him. "I will remember this moment and treasure it. You're a swell guy, Sam Finnegan."

Chapter Seventeen

With Misty at his side, Dash proudly swept back the covering to show off the ornately carved heated throne fit for a kingly Santa.

As he raised his arms and took a deep breath, and then another deep breath, while pointing to his voice box, he heard Misty say, "Will Santa Sam get his voice back? As you can see, he got his throne back. Can we cheer him on? On the count of three, can we get Silent Santa to belch out a gigantic ho, ho, ho?"

She really knew how to work a crowd, that Misty. So perfect for him.

Dash was really hamming it up, holding his belly and making like he was blowing through his lips. The crowd counted, "One."

He made a puff.

They counted, "Two."

He made a louder huff and combined it with a burp.

Laughter rippled through the mass of people, but the strange wizard woman wasn't smiling. She pointed her snowflake wand at him and her mouth moved as if cursing him.

They yelled, "Three."

It happened so fast he wasn't sure what hit him.

Dash let out a howl. Someone tackled him, knocking the wind out of him, and a trapdoor opened beneath his feet. Somewhere above him, Misty screamed.

He cursed as he fell onto a pile of hay. The trapdoor closed, and he was stuck in the dark. Above him, feet stomped and a loud, "ho, ho, ho" boomed out like thunder from Mt. Olympus.

A roar arose from the audience shouting, "Bravo. Santa's back."

"Wait, wait. I'm down here." Dash pounded on the platform above him but to no avail. No one, not even Misty, could hear him over the applause above.

He sat down and almost fell through the rim of the toilet, which had its seat raised.

Dash smashed the seat and lid down and stomped his curly-toe booted foot.

He'd told Darlene to arrange for his disappearance, but he hadn't wanted it to happen so suddenly. Now, he was stuck in his own doing.

He could not go back up there as *Sam*. Not when Dash was needed to run the show. But would Misty forgive him for disappearing? Maybe she'd believe it was part of the act.

He waited until the coast was clear, which took a while, since Santa's Gazebo was one of the most popular attractions. Fortunately, he had a toilet to sit on while he waited.

Later, much later, when he heard the last footsteps disappear, he snuck out from the trapdoor, slunk through the darkened convention center, and called a rideshare to take him away.

He missed Misty like mad, but he had to make the switch.

All he had to do was get her to fall in love with Dash Weston. Right!

* * *

The next few days passed in a blur, and Misty didn't have time to process everything that was happening. She was rushing around, running in circles, no time to talk to her sisters, no time to wrap presents for her family, no time to bake and frost cookies with her mother, and worst of all, no time to make her world-famous, okay, Christmas Creek famous, green tomato mincemeat pie. Yes, she'd canned the mixture ahead of time, but the spices she put in made it her unique contribution, and she hadn't had time to roll out the pie crust or mix the filling.

"Misty, you haven't been home in days," her twin sister, Merry, called her on her cell phone. "Everything's going well down at Southside. I don't see why you can't come home for the real Christmas Eve and Christmas Day."

"I have to keep the plates spinning. I can't afford a day off," Misty said, glancing at her watch.

"Mom and Dad got Gordon to relent and give you a two days break. Holly threatened to break up with him for being such a jerk to you."

"I don't see a way out," Misty said, even though Mr. Weston had already introduced her to his assistant, Darlene, who was chomping on the bit to take over. "If I leave my post, someone else will take my place. I need all the referrals I can get from satisfied customers and especially from Mr. Weston."

"Everyone knows you were the one who put this all together," Merry argued. "Mr. Weston is giving you credit, and get this, Gordon's invited him to have Christmas Eve dinner with us. He thinks very highly of you, and if I'm not mistaken, he might be interested in you."

"I'm not interested in him in any way other than business," Misty insisted. "Besides, I don't know what happened to Sam. Do you think Mr. Weston drove him away?"

"I heard how his paid Santa substitute practically dragged Sam off the throne," Merry said. "I thought it was part of an act."

"So did I, but I expected him to explain it to me. Instead, he's all but disappeared. The poor man didn't even give me his cell phone number. I'm sure he must have gotten a replacement by now." She didn't want to let on how hurt she was. She'd gone back to Mrs. Claus's as soon as she could get away, and Constanza had notified her that *Sam* had moved out and was last seen getting into a taxi. He hadn't left her even a note or a card.

"Did you like him a lot?" Merry asked.

"I'll get over it. I guess it'll be okay for me to take a few days off. Hanging around Christmas Village without Sam doesn't feel very good right now," Misty admitted. "Maybe I should pay attention to Mr. Weston and see what he wants. He's invited me to San Francisco to discuss business."

"Wow! That would be a real promotion. You were always wanting to see the world," Merry said. "But I'll miss you if you leave."

"I'm not leaving yet. Oh, no, here comes Darlene. She's Mr. Weston's assistant and she's acting like she wants a promotion."

"Then you'd better butter up Mr. Weston before Darlene takes all the credit. I better go now. Talk later." Her sister hung up, and Misty took a deep breath and girded herself for the onslaught.

"Well, hello there, Miss Jolly." Darlene traipsed across the gingerbread pathway wearing a sexy ice fairy outfit. "Don't look like you swallowed a cow. I'm only here to help."

"Everything's under control," Misty said. "I'm reviewing a few issues from the first Extravaganza Episode so we can address any shortcomings and get this round perfect."

"Wonderful. Dashie told me to take the baton from you. This second episode will be greater and grander than the first."

"Yes, we all hope so," Misty said. "Shall we find a quiet place to go over the issues list and prioritize the action items?"

"Definitely. Let's do it over a cup of coffee. You look like you need a break."

Darlene took Misty by the arm the way a prison warden would. Despite being a willowy brunette with large eyes and long, lush hair, she was solidly built and stronger than she looked.

After ordering and picking up their coffee, they found a table in the corner of the busy cafe. Darlene waited until Misty had finished her chocolate bear claw and drank half her coffee before launching into business.

"Dashie is so thrilled with what you've done here, and he wants me to learn all about it so we can replicate this experience worldwide. If you had to do this all over again, what is the one thing that you'd attribute your success to?"

Misty hated the way she called her boss Dashie, but it wasn't her business.

"Mr. Weston wants to speak to me about expanding themed-shopping worldwide," Misty said. "I'm excited about the prospect, but I honestly don't believe we should cookie-cut each of the Christmas Villages to duplicate what we have here at Christmas Creek."

"Why is that?" Darlene placed her cell phone on the table. "You don't mind if I record you, do you?"

"No, if it's to help Weston International, but at this point, I don't have much to offer other than what I learned doing this particular event."

"By all means, please explain. Dashie is very interested in your ideas."

"Like I said, a large part of the success we had here is due to our town traditions. We've been celebrating Christmas as a town for over fifty years when my grandfather converted the dying timber mill town into a Christmas fantasy land. What we've done at Christmas Village is to emulate the traditions of Christmas Creek and condense them into a climate-controlled, indoor, and accessible location. However, other towns and locations might have different traditions. Simply replicating Christmas Creek everywhere with the Gala Ball, the Sock Hop, the Hunky Dunky Musical Chairs, and all the rest of what we've been doing here might not work elsewhere."

"Are you holding out on me?" Darlene's heavily mascaraed eyelashes narrowed. "Dashie thinks very highly of you. Are you saying you can't weave this magic elsewhere?"

"I didn't say that. You asked me what is the one reason I believe this Christmas Village was a success and I'm conveying to you that the reason is Christmas Creek. Our town is known as a Christmas-celebrating town. Our people are supportive and have been donating their time and expertise in making this run. My sisters did the decorations and the sets. My brothers put together the northern light show, and my parents as well as the mayor and town council encouraged people to volunteer and help out, despite the Village competing with their own businesses."

Darlene scribbled something in her notebook. "So you're saying that we won't be able to replicate your success?"

"Not saying anything like that," Misty countered. "Except we have to get local buy-in and customize the experience to compliment the location. Cookie-cutter won't work. That's what all the big box stores and fast-food restaurants did. Large chain stores where everything looked the same. Chain restaurants with the same boring menus. Malls with the same department stores, the same movie theaters, playing the same movies. In order to entice people out of their homes, we need to make each experience unique. The Omaha, Nebraska, Christmas Village can't be the same as this one. The Boca Raton, Florida, one has to have their local flavor. It'll cost more, but I can imagine handing tourist-shoppers a passport where they can collect stickers from each experience, rather than they've been to one and there's no need to go to another one."

"Wow, you're brilliant. No wonder my brother is in love with you."

"Excuse me?" Misty jolted at the disconnect. "Who's your brother?"

"Oh my!" Darlene covered her mouth. "I misspoke. Delete what you heard."

"If someone's in love with me, I have a right to know," Misty said. "Is your brother Sam Finnegan? Because if he is, I want you to tell me where he's gone and whether he's okay. He paid for the full three-day First Episode and I haven't seen head nor tail of him after that sumo wrestling Santa knocked him through a trapdoor and then had the audacity of accusing him of stealing and returning the throne."

Darlene turned all shades of red and shook her head so hard, Misty was worried she was having a convulsion. She grabbed her cell phone and turned off the voice recording app.

"Let's go over the action items," she said. "Dashie is going to have my hide if I screw up the second episode."

"I don't have to hand it over to you. I can stay on. It is my gig," Misty said, liking Darlene less and trusting her not at all.

"Sorry. Mr. Weston's orders," Darlene said. "He wants you freed up so he can take you to the real Gala Ball at Gordon's mansion. Your family already invited him to Christmas Eve dinner, so I don't see how you'll get out of this."

"Uh, Darlene, I have news for you." Misty pushed her clipboard at Darlene. "I don't work for Mr. Weston. Not yet, and maybe I never will. I work for Gordon who is Mr. Weston's business partner."

"Same difference. Gordon is giving you a few days off so you can show Mr. Weston around town. He's eager for this partnership to work."

"I can show him around, but I'm not dating him. Let me make that clear." Misty glared at the hapless assistant. "Mr. Weston might be a powerful man at Weston International, but outside of work, he has no business hemming in on my personal life. I'm already seeing someone, and I don't date more than one guy at a time."

"Let me guess." A sneaky smile slithered on Darlene's face. "You're in love with the dentist, Sam Finnegan."

"That's none of your business." Misty tapped the pages on the clipboard. "This meeting is over if we're not going over the action items."

* * *

Dash watched the multiple screens in the security room high above the convention center. Not only could he see every nook and cranny of Christmas Village, but he had only to look through the one-way glass below his feet to watch Santa's Gazebo, the Candy Cane trail, the gift shops, the petting zoo, and the Christmas train chugging around the Christmas tree.

He spotted Darlene hurrying Misty into the Gingerbread Cafe, but his hackles were up when Misty charged out of the cafe without a backward glance. Darlene trotted out after her, but Misty looked angry enough to burst into a china shop and do major damage.

Unable to stop Misty, Darlene threw her hands up, looked at the glasswork above her, and even though she couldn't see through the one-way glass, she locked eyes and shrugged.

Dash called her. "What happened with Misty?"

"She's in love with Sam Finnegan and is refusing to go to the Gala Ball with you. She asked if I'm Sam's sister and wanted to know what happened to him and why she hadn't heard from him."

"Then tell her you are Sam's sister," Dash said. "Tell her he had another shock."

"Are you crazy? She's in love with Sam. She's not going to be so easily charmed by you."

"Sam is a figment of her imagination. He's mild-mannered, shy, and retiring, has shaggy gray hair, a scraggly goatee, wears dorky glasses, and is a dentist for crying out loud. I'm the CEO of Weston International."

"Well, I have news for you. She likes that mild-mannered, shy, retiring, dorky dentist with the shaggy dog look. If you're smart, you'd better contact her as Sam and reassure her that you're okay. She thinks the Santa substitute did something to him."

"You're right. I do miss her. Watching her from the eye in the sky is not the same as working next to her."

"Then why don't you make a comeback? I've a feeling she'll be real glad to see you."

"It's only putting off the inevitable," Dash said. "I can't go on being Sam the rest of my life."

"You're the CEO. You figure it out."

Chapter Eighteen

Misty spent the day before Christmas Eve with her sisters, Merry, Holly, and Ivy. The weather was relatively mild, and they strolled down Main Street and hit Brockman's General Store for last-minute gifts and stocking stuffers.

The theme for this year's Gala Ball was a very Western Christmas, and cowboy hats of all sizes, colors, and materials were flying off the shelves along with boots and fringed buckskin jackets dyed red with white trim. Holly and Ivy had matching western shirts made, one trimmed with dark glossy holly leaves and shiny red berries, and the other one with graceful curls of ivy on a white background. They wore red and green jeans and packed six-shooters in their white leather holsters.

Misty and Merry were going as dance hall or saloon girls. Both of them had spent the summer in front of the sewing machine stitching up ruffled skirts with layers of petticoats. Misty's dress was light blue like the sky with glittery white fringe on the hem of the bell-shaped skirt. The bodice was cut low, exposing arms and shoulders, and decorated with crystals and white sequins for a frosty appearance.

Merry went for a Santa-red outer dress with white fur trim. Long glittery white gloves up to her elbows contrasted with her bare arms and shoulders, and should she kick up her heels, green petticoats would bedazzle the man she chose to make merry with. She added a red pillbox hat with white trim. "This one will match perfectly."

Misty tried on a white one and selected a sky-blue ribbon to go with it. "Should I add a red feather?"

"Definitely. You'd want Sam to be able to pick you out in the crowd." Merry picked through the various accessories and bling in the bargain bin. "Look at this Indian bead band. I can use it as a choker."

Misty picked out a feathered boa and garters to go with her tights. "I'm not sure Sam is coming to the Gala Ball."

"No word?" Merry twirled a toy gun. "He didn't even let you know he was leaving?"

"I knew he would leave, but I didn't think it would be so soon," Misty said. "I keep going over everything I said and did. I don't know if I insulted him. I was so busy that last day before the grand opening and he was so helpful. Maybe I didn't thank him enough."

"Meaning?" Merry gave her an assessing look. "Did he expect you to sleep with him?"

"No, he's not that type of guy. Maybe I came on too strong when I told him to take a heart's leap with me. I don't think I said any *L* word other than like. Do you think I scared him away?"

"Might be hard for him to not be able to talk. Maybe he went home to see a doctor."

"I keep wondering if his brain injury got worse. I should have insisted he stay with Dr. Dale." Misty's stomach curdled and she felt sick. For some reason, she didn't want to admit *Sam* was speaking. What if he'd fooled her the entire time, pretending he was mute? "What have I done? He wouldn't have crashed if I hadn't distracted him."

"You don't know that. He never told Brad you were at fault. Maybe he left because he doesn't want to speak to Brad."

"Brad's right behind you." The town sheriff emerged from behind the men's row with a pair of red leather chaps trimmed with white fur. "What's this about you causing Sam Finnegan to crash his plane?"

"Misty didn't cause the crash," Merry said. "He's lucky she was nearby and able to save him."

"I still want Sam's version of the story," Brad said. "You're telling me he skipped town?"

Misty nodded, feeling even more miserable. "He didn't leave a note or anything. Just disappeared after the Santa reveal. I guess it hit him hard that Mr. Weston hired another Santa to take his place. Constanza saw him get into a taxicab and leave."

"Whose cab? Tanner or Donner?"

"What does it matter?" Merry asked. "He left Misty with a broken heart."

"Did not." Misty crossed her arms. "I'm just concerned is all."

"Uh-huh." Brad nodded with the demeanor of a disbelieving lawman. "Since he's gone, I'll let you in on another missing piece of the puzzle. Remember I told you Sam was flying someone else's plane? It turns out the airplane he crashed is registered to Mr. Dash Weston."

Misty felt the blood drain her face. "He was flying Mr. Weston's plane?"

"Yes, he was," Brad confirmed. "When I called Mr. Weston, his assistant said Sam had permission to fly it. She sent the insurance agent, and they've already picked up the pieces of the airplane. It gets even more interesting."

"What do you mean?" Misty was aghast. "Why didn't Sam tell me he knew Mr. Weston?"

"Gordon's convinced someone is spying for Mr. Weston." Merry turned toward Misty, clutching her arm. "What if Sam's the spy?"

Misty stared at her twin sister. "No, no. Sam's not a spy. He's too confused to be a spy. He took the plane because he wanted to see Christmas Village and help out."

"There has to be a crime in there somewhere," Brad said, thumbing through his notebook. "Impersonating a dentist, crashing a plane, and pulling that disappearing act. I wonder what Mr. Weston has to say about this Sam character."

"There's another explanation," Misty said, mainly to deflect the police while she figured it out. "Sam and Dash are twins. They have different colored hair and beards, but their voices sound the same."

"You're right!" Merry picked it up. "Just like no one can tell me and you apart on the phone means we can impersonate each other."

"I can tell my Ivy from Gordon's Holly," Brad said in a smug tone.

"But Ivy is more soft-spoken than Holly on purpose," Misty said. "Merry and me, we have the same chipmunk voices."

"You might call it chipmunk," Merry squeaked. "I call my voice soprano."

She hit a high note and Misty joined in, despite her heart crumbling into teeny tiny pieces.

* * *

Dash stared at the new burner phone he bought at the General Store. Unbeknownst to Merry, Misty, and that nosy Sheriff Brad Wing, he'd been hiding in the pet section of the General Store with his nose inside a barrel of kibble.

Misty sounded miserable, and it was all he could do not to charge in there and wrap his arms around her. But not as Dash Weston. She held a torch for his Sam persona, the one he put on for mystery shopping.

"Arf, whirr, woof, grrrr." Westie tugged at his ankle, and he understood the dog, for dog's sake. "You've made a horrible mess. I told you to come clean."

"Wrrr, woof, arr, ruff." Dash was shocked he could speak dog. "You're my guardian angel. Do something."

"Woof, yap, yip, aarf," Westie said. "You're Mr. Weston. You figure it out."

"Arrgh!" Dash did the only thing he could. He texted Misty.

Dash: *Hey, it's me. Sam. Sorry I didn't get a chance to say goodbye. My family's been worried about me, and when they saw me get kicked out of Santa's Gazebo, they told me to see a doctor.*

"Waahroo," Westie said. "Liar."

"Hey, you can't read," Dash grumbled. He continued to text, knowing Misty was unlikely to reply.

Dash: *I hope you are doing okay. My brother says you're top of the game. He's interested in hiring you to be head of new business development. I'm excited for you and think this is a great opportunity. You should get to know him. Don't worry about me. I'm just glad I got a chance to know you.*

The burner phone chimed with an incoming text.

Misty: *Sam, is this really you? How do I know you are who you say you are?*

Dash: *Because I went skinny-skating with you and took a Heart's Leap with you. Are you saying you took a Heart's Leap with someone else?*

Misty: *No, I never did, but did I scare you? I tend to rush into things without thinking.*

Dash: *Same here, and no, you didn't scare me. I feel the same way about you. You're the most exciting, exhilarating, and extraordinary woman I've ever met. It was worth falling out of the sky to meet you.*

Misty: *I'm glad we met, but are you okay? What did the doctor say?*

Dash: *That I have to go to a rest home for a couple of months. I didn't tell you because I was scared. I have a bad case of nerves and I pretend to be someone I'm not. It's easier than admitting I'm a little strange. I'm sorry.*

Misty: *No need to be sorry. I like you just the way you are, even if you aren't a dentist. Will you be back for Christmas?*

Dash: *No, but I'd still very much want to meet you for New Year's Eve. My nerves should be better by then. Meanwhile, my brother wants to interview you. You should take up the opportunity. I gave him my recommendation, for what it's worth.*

Misty: *Oh, Sam, you shortchange yourself. I don't know the exact nature of your issues, but I'm sure you'll get better. All I know is you're a sweet man who's guileless and good. As for your brother, he seems too aggressive, but then, he is the big boss, so I'd better make sure he's pleased with my work. Thanks for the good word from you. It means a lot.*

Dash: *My brother will take good care of you. He's really good to me and helps me with everything. I'm sorry I lied to you. It's hard to have an accomplished brother and be nothing compared to him.*

Misty: *You are NOT nothing, but I understand. My sisters are so much more accomplished than me. Holly has her own business, and Ivy is the Chamber of Commerce here, as well as an interior decorator and set designer. They have great boyfriends, as you know, and I might have put too much pressure on you by acting as if you were my boyfriend. I deserved to be fooled, thinking you were a dentist and that I could brag about it. I'm the one who should be sorry. Let's start over as friends and see where it goes.*

Dash: *What about that heart's leap we took? Was that real even if I'm not who I say I am?*

Misty: *It was real, or at least I wished it to be. I wanted so much to have a boyfriend that I rushed in like a fool. In the back of my mind I knew you'd be leaving, but I wanted to make more of it than you were ready for.*

Dash: *Don't blame yourself. I, too, wanted more than meets the eye. If we could have another chance, will you grant me a wish and take it slower?*

Misty: *Sure. Let's see what happens New Year's Eve. I hope you are well rested and over your shock by then.*

Dash: *That gives me hope. I'll do everything the doctor says, but I'll understand if you like my brother better. Women always do.*

Misty: *I'm not an ordinary woman. You said so yourself. I'm exciting, exhilarating, and extraordinary.*

Dash: *That you are. Merry Christmas, Misty.*

Misty: *Merry Christmas to you too. Keep in touch.*

Dash: *I will. Oh, I will.*

Chapter Nineteen

On Christmas Eve, Misty spent a jolly day with her family. They served a delightful Christmas breakfast at the homeless shelter, enacted a play about a lost and found Christmas elf with Westie making a surprise appearance, and then went door to door passing out Christmas treats to their neighbors. After lunch, the Jolly kitchen was a hubbub of activity. While Mom wrapped the holiday ham, Holly made the macaroni and cheese while Ivy shaped the cheese balls and molded salads. Everyone wore their Gala Ball costumes, and it was hard to keep the flour out of their hair and sauces from splattering their gay outfits, but as a diehard Jolly, they had no time to change once the festivities started.

Misty's hair was pulled up into a fancy updo which she tied up inside a bandana. She wore an apron to protect her saloon girl dress, and she finally had time to roll out pie dough and fill it with her green tomato mincemeat mixture while Merry hummed around the kitchen to "It's the Most Wonderful Time of the Year." Meanwhile, Mick's girlfriend, Kitty, was busily mixing the spices that would go into the mulled wine while her cat, Figgy, hissed and swiped at Holly's dog, Rudolph, every time he stuck his nose onto the counter.

The benefit of being in a large family was plenty of distraction and activity. Misty had no time to be lonely despite the ache in her heart. Had she rushed into something that wasn't there? Was it her wishful thinking that made her fall head over heels for a man who barely spoke? She'd projected her own desire for companionship on to *Sam*. Still, he seemed to have enjoyed her company, and the kisses he gave her bordered on hot and wanting more.

She pressed the pie dough into a pocket pie mold. She was making individual tarts so there'd be no fighting over the favorite family dessert. She'd used her green tomato mincemeat pie as a test for boyfriend compatibility. Would *Sam* eat it with gusto or turn his nose up at it? She'd bet he'd love it. The man loved everything about Christmas. Too bad he was missing out on Christmas Eve with her at Jolly Ranch.

Outside, the boys were chopping wood and shaking snow off the wreaths and lights. Gordon and Dash were meeting in Dad's study with Darlene to go over the Southside issues and action items. Why wasn't she included? Was this part of pushing her aside? Telling her she, the local girl, was done and transferring everything to Dash's assistant?

"What's wrong?" Merry nudged her hip. "You look like you're concentrating hard on the pie crust. Thinking about Sam?"

Misty blinked back the tears that came so easily these days. "I know he was only a visitor, but we were so compatible. He loved Christmas as much as anyone in our family. Actually, he might have loved it more. I keep thinking about him living at the rest home and being stuck with the fake holiday cheer they foist on patients. When Dash said he couldn't have booked a Christmas Village reservation so early, I almost wonder if he forged the reservation and planned the big getaway only to get caught. What if Dash has him committed to a mental hospital?"

"Oh, Misty, you'll have to ask Dash about this. It's the height of cruelty to keep such a beautiful and innocent soul from Christmas magic."

Misty wiped her eyes with the back of her floured hand. "I know. I should have fought off that wrestler Santa. I thought it was an act, and now Sam's gone forever."

Throats clearing at the kitchen entrance startled Misty. Gordon, Dash, and Darlene held clipboards and electronic tablets, clearly making a survey or observing the whirlwind of activity—no doubt to steal ideas for future Christmas projects.

Misty turned her back on them.

"May I help you?" Merry piped up in a falsely cheerful squeak at the interlopers. "Something to drink? Eggnog? Cider? The mulled wine isn't ready yet."

"We're admiring a real farmhouse kitchen," Darlene said while Gordon went and put his arms around Holly. "It's amazing how coordinated you are. What are you making?"

"I'm roasting vegetables for the side dishes," Holly said. "Mom has the pastry-wrapped ham ready to bake. Misty is making her world-famous green tomato mincemeat pie with her secret ingredient."

"You're all invited to dinner," Mom said. "Didn't you say your dad and aunt are in town?"

"Aunt Sharky is whipping up a Christmas meatloaf and stollen rolls at the test kitchen," Dash said. "She's putting on a demonstration of Christmas Eve recipes for the visitors."

"Invite your entire family," Mom said. "We have plenty of food, and I know Gordon is thrilled that everyone's here."

"Everyone except Sam," Misty muttered and shot Dash a hostile glare. "Are you embarrassed of him? Because we Jollys like Sam, even with his issues."

"Misty!" Mom scolded. "I'm sure there are good reasons for Sam to rest. He barely survived the plane crash."

"Thanks to me!" Misty's lower lip wobbled as tears threatened to burst. "I'm not going to the Gala Ball as long as Sam is under house arrest."

"Don't be ridiculous," Gordon said. "Sam is overtired from all the activity you took him on. It's a miracle he didn't catch pneumonia. Constanza said his lips were blue after you dragged him to the frozen swimming hole. What did you do to him?"

"He was fine." Misty slapped the pie pastry on the counter. "He was looking forward to being Santa for all nine days."

"How did you know? He couldn't talk," Gordon said. "You're putting words in his mouth. That's how you are, Misty, running roughshod over everyone."

"Wait, you leave my sister alone," Holly said, giving him a shove. "You've been behaving badly ever since you roped Misty into this project."

"Yeah, we've put up with your airs because you practically own this town," Ivy chimed in. "My sister is concerned about Sam and so am I. Brad says Sam has a fake ID."

"Oh my, oh my." Mom wrung her hands. "What if Sam escaped from the mental hospital? It's lucky he didn't die in the plane crash."

"Sam is not a mental case!" Misty screamed. "He's a sensitive and sweet man. He loves Christmas and sees everything with the eyes of a innocent child. I'm not putting words in his mouth because guess what? He regained his voice a few days back, but no wonder he kept quiet. Everyone's against him. But not me. I'm going on strike until I find out what happened to him. And I'm going to start by interrogating Dash."

She whirled around to where he'd been standing at the kitchen door. "Mr. Weston. Oh drat. Where did Mr. Weston go?"

"Great job, Misty," Gordon said, clapping slowly. "You just insulted our biggest investor. You better hope he doesn't pull his investment or our town is bankrupt. Unlike Sam, Dash hates all things Christmas except for the profits."

"Shut up!" all the Jolly females shouted at Gordon while Misty tore off her apron and grabbed her coat and keys.

This was her worst Christmas Eve ever.

* * *

Dash was in big trouble. He was filled with regret since catching sight of Misty in the kitchen wearing her Gala Ball costume while rolling out pastry dough and trying her level best to appear normal. She was hurting, and he was the one who caused her pain. She wasn't wrong to rush into love. When the right person clicked, it would be stupid to hold back. Problem was she was in love with one of his shopping personalities and not his real stodgy, all-business identity. He hadn't gotten where he was at Weston International by being fanciful and childlike. No, he was a hard-nosed businessman more concerned about the bottom line than fairy tales and celebrations.

His lies were bubbling to the surface, but he couldn't afford to let the world know about his mystery shopping habit and the many disguises he'd perfected over the years. It was the secret of Weston International's retail success and the reason they hadn't gotten canceled by online shopping. Their in-person retail stores seemed to resonate with their target customers in a way no analyst could account for.

Sam Finnegan was only one of his repertoires, and if he was outed, he would no longer be able to mystery shop and tour the rest of his life. Who could have predicted he'd fall in love while impersonating a Christmas lover?

He ran as fast as he could across the field of the Jolly ranch toward the stables where he'd stashed his Sam Single Santa outfit. It was a stroke of luck he'd thought about surprising the guests at the Gala Ball with a reappearance, but now, with Misty going on strike, he'd have to resurrect earlier and make it up to her. What if he had to stay Sam Single forever? He couldn't lose her.

His heart hurt when her heart hurt.

Even more of a bonus, she was loyal and would never cheat on Sam. She hotly defended her friends and believed the best about them. He'd tested her by asking her to the Gala Ball as well as to a New Year's Eve meeting, but Sam was the only man she wanted.

So he'd be Sam until he could figure out how to let her in on the secret.

Dash hid behind the giant draft horses the Jollys used to pull their four-horse sleigh. A big fellow nickered and nosed him, hoping for a treat. Dash pulled out a carrot he stole from Merry's prep table and patted the horse while he munched on it.

Truth was Dash missed Misty too, and he needed to hold her and kiss her like he needed oxygen. He stripped out of his business clothes and pulled on Sam's red-and-white-striped sweater and the light-blue lederhosen. He encased his calves in the same red-and-white-striped stockings. Tooled leather boots and a gunslinger's belt with slots for 12-gauge shotgun shells completed his "Western" outfit.

The spirit gum was frozen, so Dash couldn't stick Sam's silver whiskers on his face, and the white wig was tangled and full of burrs. To hide his dyed dark-brown hair, he had no choice but to tie his red silk cravat over his head like a pirate. Instead of a Santa hat, he fitted himself with a bright-red leather cowboy hat with a sky-blue feather. He'd picked up a gift for Misty but had left it at the Mill Inn, so it meant a trek through fields and forest to the town square before surprising Misty at the Gala Ball.

After stowing his Dash Weston identity, including his cell phone, rental car keys, wallet, and identification—he couldn't take any chances—Dash jogged down the country lane toward the center of town. The chill breeze whipped his scarf, and his boots sank into the snow up to his knees, freezing his legs. He was huffing and puffing around a hairpin turn when the blare of a horn and the juddering sound of locked tires over ice shot his heart to his throat. He whipped his head around and froze. Misty's Jeep bore down on him. She was struggling with the steering, her eyes bulging wide and her hair a wild crown of curls over her screaming mouth. He needed to move. To jump. To dodge. To tumble. But he couldn't move. Couldn't blink. Couldn't take a breath. Couldn't move a muscle.

The Jeep skidded sideways, crashed through a split-rail fence, and spun like a wild top. It tumbled over the snow, bouncing and swerving over an entire family of snow people before jamming to a stop against a snow-covered hay maze.

"Misty!" Dash's muscles unfroze, and he was all arms and legs windmilling and sprinting after the Jeep. "Woof, wwuff, ruff."

Frantically, he yanked open the driver's door. Misty was sprawled behind the airbags. Her eyes were closed, but there was no visible blood. Remembering his CPR training, he gently unhooked her seat belt and checked her pulse. He put his lips close to hers and felt her breathe.

"Whirr, ruff, grrr, woof." He meant to call her name, but his tongue was stuck to the roof of his mouth, and the only sounds from his throat were dog.

Misty's eyes were still closed and she appeared to be sleeping. He couldn't move her in case she had spinal injuries, and he didn't have his cell phone because he'd left Dash's behind and tossed the burner Sam was using.

There was only one thing to do. It worked in fairy tales, and today was Christmas Eve. Maybe the elves would do him a favor. He caressed her face and closing his eyes, he leaned in and kissed her. Her lips were soft and cool, and thank goodness, they moved, slowly at first, tentatively, but as he inhaled her blessed breath, his relief grew and tears stung his eyes. His Misty was going to be okay, and maybe, just maybe, she would forgive him and give him a chance to right all wrongs.

He wanted to tell her he loved her, but the only sounds coming from him were tiny burrs like a purring dog, if any existed. Where was Westie when he needed him?

Her hand slid around the back of his neck and she moaned. Her eyelids fluttered against his cheek, but he kept kissing her. He had to get in every taste before she woke all the way and pushed him away. If she thought he was Dash dressed as Sam, she'd for sure slap him hard.

"Who, what, who?" she muttered, squirming beneath him.

He opened his mouth to speak, but nothing emitted other than a pleading whine.

"Wait, are you Dash or Sam?" her voice was gentle but full of doubt.

Dash opened his mouth to tell the truth. "Wrroff, yip, yap, woah."

She narrowed her eyes and shook her head slowly. "Still up to your tricks, aren't you?"

He shook his head and pointed to his mouth, desperately signaling he couldn't speak.

"You kiss like Sam," she said. "But you don't have his whiskers. Then again, you two are twins. I should be able to tell you apart. There's got to be something different like a chipped tooth or a scar."

He made a puppy face, sad that there were no distinguishable features while she explored his face with her fingers, touching the tip of his cleft chin, stroking underneath his jaw, and then checking out the hair under his red silk headband. She even touched the corners of his eyes, looking for the nonexistent crow's feet. He was a young man with prematurely gray hair. In a few days, she might see the roots, but right now, with the fresh dye job, she wouldn't see any evidence of her "Sam."

He shrugged again, asking her what she thought.

Her lips pursed and the creases between her eyes deepened as she grabbed his wrist and held his hand up. "You're not acting like a jerk, so I'm inclined to think you're Sam, but you're wearing Dash's watch."

He inhaled sharply and stared at the offending Rolex. But shouldn't he want her to believe he was Dash so he could start on the road back to her good graces?

Without warning, she pinched him.

Instead of "ow," he squeaked like a dog in pain.

"Oh, you're good. Real good." She chuckled. "I wish Westie were here. I bet he knows. He likes Sam, but Hayley at the General Store told everyone he hates Dash. She saw him lurking in the pet food aisle when Westie bit his ankle and growled at him."

Dash made motions of petting Westie, trying to convince her the dog liked him, but she only smiled and said, "Dash is worse than Gordon when it comes to hating Christmas. I'm going to take a chance that you're Sam because you're wearing the Sam Single costume. What did you do? Steal Dash's watch or guilt him into giving it to you?"

Dash didn't want to continue lying so he only smiled.

"You have perfect teeth like Sam and a smile as sweet as his," she babbled happily. "I hope you beat up that Dash and tied him up somewhere."

Dash nodded eagerly and then patted her arms and legs, making motions to ask her if she could move.

She groaned and pulled herself up, twisting her ankles and pulling down the petticoats and hem of her fringe dress that had rode up too high.

He gave her a smile and a thumbs-up, glad she was okay. Problem was, the Jeep was stuck and he wanted to get to the Mill Inn to get her gift.

"Okay, we're in a pickle," she said, gingerly trying to get out of her Jeep.

Since her tights were sheer and her boots were too short, she wasn't protected for knee-deep snow. He wrapped her in his arms and tilted his head toward the road. He'd carry her out and walk all the way back to town. As long as she loved him, he didn't care which one he was.

She opened her purse and extracted her cell phone. "I'll call for a cab. It might take a while because everyone's flocking to Southside Glen."

He nodded, and while she made the call, he walked through the snow. One foot in front of the other, step by step with his prize in his arms.

"Shouldn't we go back to my parents' place?" she asked when he headed toward town.

He shook his head slowly and placed a kiss on her cheek. He wanted her to himself, and nothing but trouble awaited him where his sister and Gordon would out him to her family.

"Oh, good, there's the taxi," she said.

A bright-red Cadillac from the old days, complete with tail fins and whitewall tires, lumbered down the lane toward them. When it pulled up to them, a wiry elf-like man wearing a red-and-green-plaid shearling jacket hopped out to open the passenger door. Bells jingled on his white fur-trimmed boots, and he wore buckskin pants with a wampum belt around his waist. A green Santa's hat hung low over his forehead, and his beard was scraggly underneath a pointy nose.

"It's Donner," Misty said. "We're in for a treat."

"You're definitely in for a treat, Miss Jolly." Donner held the door for her to crawl onto the ridged vinyl back seat devoid of seatbelts. "And who is this wonderful young gentleman?"

"He's Kris Kringle's little brother, Sam Single." Misty extended her gloved hand and pulled Dash in next to her.

"I'm Donner, no relation to the party," the elderly elf quipped with a wink. "Where to?"

"Whirr, woof, wow?" Dash asked, meaning to say, "Can you take us to Mill Inn?"

"The Mill Inn it is," Donner replied, getting back in the driver's seat.

"You can understand him?" Misty blinked with surprise. "Tell me, Donner, is he Sam or Dash?"

Dash withered under Donner's fierce stare. He held his breath until Donner flashed him a wink and put the old Cadillac in gear.

"Well?" Misty asked. "Sam and Dash are twins, and they're playing tricks on me. If you understand him, ask him which one he is. I need to know before I make even more of a fool out of myself. I rushed into something I shouldn't have, and my heart dashed into a million pieces when Sam left without a word. His mean brother spread rumors about him, and now Sam is back, but he's wearing Dash's watch and has Dash's short brown hair."

"Hold it, hold it!" Donner put his hands over his ears. "Miss Misty. You talk too fast for an old elf like me, and you drive way too fast. Sometimes, it's better to take the slow boat. Get more of the scenery and all the little details along the way."

"But I need to know before I make an even bigger fool of myself."

Donner drove as slow as a snail. Dash didn't mind because he placed his arm around Misty's shoulders and she didn't object. Oh, she'd darted him a skeptical glance, but at least she didn't elbow him.

"Why do you care if you're a fool in love?" Donner asked in a slow, creaky voice. "Love brings out the best in us, and there's no better fool than one who trusts his or her heart. What does your heart tell you?"

Dash's heart was jumping up and down, raising and waving his hand, knowing the answer. But this was Misty's heart, and she had to answer the question on her own. He snuck a kiss on her cheek and she turned toward him with a cuddle. But she was still unsure and her shoulders were stiff.

"My heart isn't speaking," Misty finally acknowledged. "I can't decide. He feels like Sam but he could also be Dash pretending to be Sam. Dash is a trickster and a liar. You know he hates Christmas and only cares about money?"

"I thought you cared about profits too," Donner said. "No profits means no jobs and no jobs means no happiness."

"But he hates Christmas and is only pretending to celebrate it. That's what everyone says."

"What does your heart say?" Donner took his hands off the steering wheel and twisted around to stare at Dash. "Sam or Dash?"

"I don't know." Misty also focused on him, and all Dash could do was wonder how the Cadillac steered itself without Donner driving.

"Ask him," Donner said. "Ask him to raise his right hand if he's Dash and his left hand if he's Sam."

"He could lie," Misty insisted.

"Then it doesn't much matter, does it?" Donner said, finally turning back to his driving. "Love means trusting and believing and taking a risk. Risk nothing, gain nothing. Risk and reward are two sides of the same coin. Two sides of the same coin, Miss Jolly."

Chapter Twenty

Misty had never had a date at the Mill Inn, despite being a Christmas Creek native. Her sister Holly used to dine there every year with Gordon's great-aunt Miss Marley because she was her protégé and keeper of the Gills family history. She'd heard about the opulent Gold Rush furnishings inside and the gold-veined stone exterior. The high-pitched roof and mullioned windows as well as its centuries old appearance gave it an authenticity not found in a theme park copy.

After Donner drove away, *Sam* offered his arm clad in a red-and-white striped sweater, and Misty realized they were woefully underdressed for the historical inn. Fortunately, it was Christmas Eve and other patrons wore costumes, so they weren't too out of place. Misty tugged and straightened her petticoat and finger-combed the fringe of her dance hall girl outfit. Her hair was a bird's nest mess, but it fit the Wild, Wild West theme.

Still, she stood up straight and flounced her skirt while walking with *Sam* into the Inn. The maître d' was seating a couple ahead of them, and they were greeted by the owner's daughter, Gina Golightly, who was the town's biggest flirt.

"Why, Mr. Weston," Gina said. "What a delightful costume. Are you going to the Gala Ball as the Cat in the Hat?"

Sam only smiled, so the flirt picked up two menus and said, "You don't have reservations, but since you're lodging here, we have a special table for you near the model sawmill. My father hired the best craftsmen to recreate this panoramic scene. If you want to include it in your Christmas Villages, he'll be glad to talk terms about licensing the concept."

Sam nodded politely and Gina took it to mean he agreed, so she chattered on. "We're recreating German Christmas market fare tonight. Our special tonight is roast goose with sides of spätzle, knödel, and red cabbage. Dessert is our scrumptious pfeffernusse cookies. Would you like to start with a pint of gluhwein? Or if you prefer, we have turbo punsch, which is fruit punch spiked with schnapps."

Sam pulled the chair back for Misty and waited for her to settle in before pushing it in place. This was such an old-fashioned courtesy, Misty couldn't recall seeing it done other than in old movies. He took a seat across the small table from her, facing the sawmill display.

"Do you have fish?" Misty asked, not wanting to get bogged down by a heavy meal.

Gina placed the menus on the table. "Of course, we do have a flavorful carp with potato salad on the side, or the smoked peppercorn salmon with potato pancakes."

"I'll take the salmon," Misty said. "Sam?"

"Oh, I get what's going on," Gina said. "Mr. Weston is pretending to be Sam Finnegan, the dentist who crash-landed at our airport. I heard he suffered a real shock and disappeared the day of the grand opening."

Sam shot her a closemouthed smile and turned his attention to the menu, so Misty said, "He needs more time to order."

"Mr. Weston told me last night he wanted to try the beef roulades with red cabbage," Gina said. "Why don't I put that in for you?"

Sam nodded and Gina collected the menus and departed with a superior smirk as if she was in on a secret.

Misty kept her doubts to herself. While Dash might have stayed at the Mill Inn the previous night, there was no way the sophisticated Dash Weston would risk being seen in *Sam's* lederhosen Cat in the Hat outfit. Gina had simply mistaken the twins, and *Sam* was too polite, as well as tongue-tied, to contradict her. All the more proof the humble man sitting across from her had to be her *Sam*.

Holding up her hand, she pressed her palm to *Sam's*.

"I owe you an apology," she said while gazing adoringly into his eyes. "I shouldn't have accused you of playing tricks on me and asking Donner to quiz you. It's just coincidence that Dash was at my family's home with Gordon, making an ass out of himself. I was trying to get as far away from him as I could, and I almost plowed into you, and then I go and accuse you of being Dash. Will you forgive me for doubting?"

Sam lowered his gaze, picked up her hand, and pressed a soft kiss onto it. The corners of his mouth turned down woefully, and she was sure she'd hurt his feelings.

"When you get your voice back, I want to hear all about what Dash and that monstrous Santa he hired did to you. And look at this." She extracted her cell phone and brought up the text messaging app. "He made you send these text messages, didn't he? Telling me you were going to a rest home and encouraging me to go on a date with him."

Sam stared at the patterns on the tablecloth. Guilt was written all over his face. He wouldn't meet her gaze, and he kept pursing and unpursing his lips.

"Oh, there I go again, accusing you. I'm sorry." She put away her phone. "I know how it is with twins. One twin is usually dominant and can take things too far. Holly lords over Ivy, and even though I hate to admit it, I talk five times as much as Merry and growing up, I was always putting words in her mouth." She took his hand and caressed it. "I'll wait until you get your voice back so you can defend yourself. Whatever you suffered, I'll take it up with Dash. None of this is your fault. I know you meant well, because you wanted me to get a business deal and you thought Dash could advance my career. Except I'm not walking over you to do that. Do you still care about me like you did when we took that heart's leap?"

His genuine smile brightened his masculine face, and Misty took that as an affirmative. Her *Sam* still felt the same way about her as he did that night and the next day when he so excitedly helped her with the grand opening. Her heart leaped again at the bit of Christmas magic that had her Jeep almost mowing him down.

"Let's enjoy this evening and everything that goes with Christmas," she said. "You've never seen anything like the real Gala Ball. If you love Christmas as much as I do, it'll be one of the happiest evenings of your life. This year is a very Western Christmas, but last year we had the Nutcracker with a real Drosselmeyer, well, I'll let you in on a secret. Gordon was a lot nicer last year because he didn't have all this pressure, and he played Herr Drosselmeyer, the toymaker who made all the dolls, toy soldiers, and windup animals. You should have seen the costumes. We had ice princes and princesses, ballerinas, Russian Cossacks, toy soldiers galore, dancing bears, and lots of rat-faced minions. I was a sugar-frosted fairy, and Merry was a cream puff pixie."

Sam only smiled and held her hand, beaming at her with lovesick eyes.

That decided it. How could she have ever doubted his obvious love for Christmas?

Dash Weston could never fake so much Christmas cheer.

"I hope you win the costume contest and they crown you the Christmas King. Then I'd get to go to the Sock Hop with the King of Christmas and you can wear your crown proudly the entire Christmas Day."

Standing up, he leaned across the small table and kissed her, clearly sealing his wish to be all things Christmas.

Yes!

Donner was right. Love and trust were two sides of the same coin.

* * *

Dash wanted his voice back too. Not only to set things straight, but to tell Misty how much she meant to him. But for now, he had only one chance to make it right. He had to open his mind and see Christmas through *Sam's* wondering eyes.

Why was it he could pretend to be Sam and sit inside an entirely Christmasfied dining room and actually appreciate the decor as well as the happy sounds of people enjoying a holiday meal? The wood-paneled dining room was filled with wreathes and candles, and the potted fir trees were tastefully decorated with antique ornaments made from wood, metals, and glass. As for the sawmill diorama, it included a complete miniature forest made of wood and a self-feeding fountain where water flowing down the river ended in a glass-bottomed lake. Tiny logs were arranged on the flume down to a log pond. Snow-capped mountain peaks rose above the mill, and miniature lumberjacks were arranged around the trees.

Misty stood from her seat and tapped his arm. "While we're waiting, let's take a tour and check out the hallway displays. Mr. Golightly consulted with my grandfather and my father on the settings."

Dash eagerly took her hand and even though he'd rushed through the hall leading to the rooms the night before, this time, he studied each arrangement of Christmas artifacts depicting the history of Christmas as it was celebrated from the founding of the Mill Inn.

"Incredible, isn't it?" Misty pointed to a stunning snow angel ornament. "They spent so much time with the glass, scraps of lace, beads, trim, and teeny tiny paintbrushes. Look at the cherubic expression on her face."

Dash wanted to add his observations, but he only hummed with appreciation and peered closer at the old-fashioned printed scraps of paper that depicted holiday scenes. He pointed to a glittery blue glass bird with a spun-glass tail sitting on a silver glass bell trimmed with dark-green holly leaves and red berries. The edge of the bell was decorated with lace and fringe, and tinsel hung from the wired handle.

"Which display do you like most?" Misty asked.

He smiled and walked across to a collection of Santa figurines. They certainly depicted the old elf differently back in the day. For one thing, he was quite thin and had a serious expression. He was heavily laden with trees and bags of toys, and in some of the pictures, he wore a bishop's miter. A few had red robes, but most of the Father Christmas figures wore tan, green, or brown furs. The hoods to keep them warm eventually turned into the triangular Santa hat, and there was one with a cowboy hat.

Dash pointed to the cowboy Santa who was wearing a blue denim overall and then hooked a thumb at himself. Teddy bears and dolls peeked out of the bib of the overalls, and the Santa was carrying a silver puppy dog.

"That's you, Sam," Misty said. "And Westie. I wonder where he went after he bit Dash at the General Store."

Dash shrugged and put on an innocent look. He wasn't lying because he didn't know where Westie had gone.

They stopped to admire a display of antique Christmas trees made of painted ostrich feathers, and by the time they finished studying the Gold Rush painting of Saturnalia celebrated in a saloon, complete with booze, dancing girls, and card games, their meals were ready.

Their dishes were garnished with sprigs of rosemary and tiny peppermints wrapped with gilded ribbons. Soft instrumental music played in the background. The mulled wine was warm and scented, and the food was tasty. But what had Dash's heart reeling and tumbling into the Christmas Creek was a combination of Misty's delightful laughter, spirited commentary, and radiant beauty. If it weren't for Christmas, none of this would have happened, and he would not be head over heels in love with his very own Christmas angel.

He just had to make it right before she found out the truth.

Chapter Twenty-One

After dinner, Misty and *Sam* caught a ride on Mayor Tompkins' sleigh on their way to Gordon's mansion for the Gala Ball. They had been dining at the Mill Inn and happened to step out at the same time.

"We're so absolutely tickled pink to have you in town," Mrs. Tompkins said to *Sam* in her grandiose manner. "Imagine the CEO of Weston International spending his Christmas holidays here in our nook of the woods."

Sam smiled but did not reply.

"How do you like our little town?" Mayor Tompkins asked. "I haven't been down to Southside yet, but can anything compare to the Mill Inn and the Victorian mansions of Town Square?"

Again, *Sam* nodded and smiled.

"Uh, I hate to interrupt," Misty said. "But this is Sam Finnegan. He's the dentist who crashed his plane. He had a shock and is trying to get his speech back."

"Oh, that's awful," Mrs. Tompkins said. "But other than the Sam Single Santa costume, you look just like Dash Weston. Why, there's even that shaving cut that was bleeding when we had dinner the night of the grand opening."

"Harriet, you notice too much," the mayor said. "It looks like Sam shaved off his goatee too. Now, I'm one of the judges for the Christmas King contest. Misty knows what it is, but it's for the best dressed Santa or Father Christmas. You're going to have some stiff competition, but it's real gutsy of you to go clean-shaven on Santa."

"I happened to like a clean-shaven Santa," Mrs. Tompkins pronounced. "Good luck to you, Sam. I wonder if Dash will give you a run for your money."

"Dash is unlikely to dress up," the mayor said. "He's probably over at Southside Glen counting his profits. The sheriff told me the traffic jam is legendary. Apparently, they're going to rival our Gala Ball by putting on a fireworks show."

"A Christmas fireworks show?" Misty gasped. "How come I didn't know about this?"

A sour feeling squeezed her stomach. But of course. Dash brought in his assistant, Darlene, to take over. From the sound of it, Aunt Sharky would displace Constanza as Mrs. Claus, and Dash's father could even be the new and improved Santa Claus, shoving aside Chief Rumsey.

Sam tugged her tighter into his arm and gave her a reassuring kiss on the side of her head. At least he was on her side, but still, what a disappointment if the Southside Gala Ball drew more people than the traditional one.

A jolt of fear shot through her as she craned her neck at the road down toward Southside. It was jam-packed, and that could explain why the town residents were riding their horses and using their sleighs and snowmobiles to avoid the roads.

What if no one showed up to the Gala Ball other than the mayor and her family?

* * *

"Whirr, woo, woof," Dash coughed in a low voice once they arrived at the Gills Mansion. When was he going to get his voice back?

Misty's assumptions were digging him deeper and deeper into a pit. When the mayor's wife commented on his shaving nick, he was sure Misty would have twigged to him being Dash instead of Sam.

And then there was Misty's exclamation of not knowing about the fireworks show at Southside. It was Darlene's idea, and he'd approved it. Darlene had pointed out that their job wasn't only to replicate what Christmas Creek had, but to improve on it and provide additional wow experiences.

Still, Misty looked disappointed and there was nothing he could do but hug her tight.

Once they entered the mansion, the mayor introduced him to most of the townsfolk he hadn't had a chance to meet. They all thought of him as Sam, and a few of them jokingly opened their mouths wide and asked him to look at their teeth. Misty's family was arrayed among the sawdust and hay bales decorating the ballroom to make it look like a hoedown barn.

"You made it!" one of her brothers who was wearing a coonskin hat and buckskin said. "When you drove off so fast, we didn't know where you were going."

"I found Sam." She took Dash's hand and cuddled against him.

"That's great," Holly said. "Gordon's worried sick about Dash. Did you see him?"

"No, but I don't particularly care," Misty said. "He has his assistant taking over my job, and they're doing everything they can to take people away from us. Did you know they're having fireworks?"

"I heard about that," Ivy said. "Poor Brad is so busy with the traffic jams, I don't think he'll make it, but Dad says we can head over on the four-horse sleigh before midnight and see it."

"Before midnight? No way," Misty said. "That's when we crown the Christmas King."

The buckskin brother glanced around the mostly empty ballroom. "Either everyone's stuck in traffic, or our turnout is less than last year."

"We're still nominating the Christmas King here, even if all the Santa wannabes went to Southside," Misty huffed. "Sam's competing. He can't be the only one."

"Ho, ho, ho." A large man resembling a wilderness Santa wearing fur pelts lapped his hands. "Welcome one and welcome all to Christmas Creek's first ever Christmas Hoedown. Now, if you all will put your hands together, let's hear from Mayor Tompkins and get this gig started."

A flurry of fiddles sawing away heralded the mayor who stood upon a hay bale. He was wearing a large white cowboy hat, and an old-fashioned suit of clothes—not looking very Christmassy at all.

A bevy of cowgirls passed around eggnog and spiced cider, and after the mayor introduced the square dance caller, the fiddlers improvised a rousing "Jingle Bells/We Wish You a Merry Christmas" set, and soon everyone grabbed partners and swung around the square.

Despite the sparse crowd, Dash was enjoying himself and glad that he was finally putting his eighth-grade gym class moves to work. He swung Misty around in a do-si-do and exchanging partners as they went, he danced with her sisters, and switched off with her brothers. They two-stepped around the Christmas tree and galloped to "Up on the Housetop." Everyone wore sleigh bells and did the Jingle Bell polka. Maybe the Gala Ball wasn't like the year before when they'd done the Nutcracker theme, but this was special and different and the only one that mattered to Dash.

The fiddlers outdid themselves combining Christmas songs with "Turkey in the Straw" and other old-time fiddling tunes, and everyone had fun skipping around the ballroom barn on stick ponies and lassoing each other.

Misty was the belle of the ball as far as he was concerned. Her sky-blue ruffled dress swung high when she spun around and strutted every jut of her womanly curves. The cloud of soft curls floated around her cover model face, and the sparkle in those true-blue eyes of hers shone with joy and happiness. She and her town sure knew how to make merry, whether line dancing or waltzing.

The slow dances to a cowboy guitar and western rendition of "Santa Baby" had Misty melting in his arms, and the long, long kisses, well, Dash put every ounce of love into them. He needed to let her know without words how he'd changed from a Christmas profiteer to a diehard Christmas lover.

Everything was magical, from the red-and-green sprinkles on the hoofprint cookies to the peppermint bark or as Mrs. Jolly called them, peppermint cow turds, to the cinnamon and spice funnel cakes, and all the horseshoes tacked on the walls with holly, ribbons, and tinsel hanging off them showed Dash that Christmas wasn't in the money but the spirit of love, family, and goodwill to all mankind.

When he fell with Misty onto a pile of hay, he held her tight, rolling over her and kissing the life out of her.

"This is the best Christmas I've ever had, and it's all thanks to you," he said as the grandfather clock started to chime in the background.

"Sam, you're talking! Oh my, that's the best gift ever."

"I have to tell you," he began.

"No, me first. I love you, Sam." She pressed a lingering kiss on his lips that lasted eight chimes.

"I have to tell you," he stuttered. "I'm not Sam, but I love Christmas and I love—"

The last chime rang and his words were drowned out by the big trapper guy's voice booming through the speakers. "Merry Christmas!"

The entire barn, or ballroom, erupted with whistles and cheers, and everyone turned to kiss their partners. Misty's eyes were large and confused, and Dash had to rush to explain.

"I'm Dash. I've always been Dash, but now, I'm also Sam. I know why he loves Christmas, and it's because he loves you."

"Ho, ho, ho!" a man's voice boomed. "Now is the moment we've all be waiting for. Mayor Tompkins will announce the new Christmas King of our very Western Christmas Gala!"

"I don't get it." Misty's brow crinkled. "How can you be your twin brother?"

"I was a mystery shopper. Sam is one of my personalities. But you can't tell anyone. It's a Weston International trade secret. We mystery shop and tour so we can improve our retail experiences."

She gave him a hard push. "You were spying on us?"

"Hey, there's fireworks at Southside," a woman's voice said. "They're live-streaming it. That's where all the people went."

"Ho, ho, ho." The deep-voiced man valiantly tried to get attention. "Now, the mayor."

No one paid attention, as the remaining Christmas cowboys and cowgirls lit up their cell phones and oohed and aahed to the fireworks show going on at Southside.

"I hate you." Misty's glare shot daggers at him. "You stole my ideas and sent your assistant to take over. Then you distracted me with Sam and pretended you couldn't talk to keep the truth from me. Now, everyone's at Southside."

"Let me explain," Dash pleaded. "I didn't—"

The mayor tapped the microphone and announced, "We had two contestants for Christmas King. Nick Jolly, the trapper Santa and Sam Finnegan, the farmer Santa. It was close, believe me, but this year's Christmas King is none other than the man who fell from the sky, Dr. Sam Finnegan. Come up here, Dr. Sam, for your crown. Speaking of crowns, one of mine is loose, and all of us have sweet tooths here, and we really could use a dentist, especially my wife, Harriet, who needs a bridge. Put your hands together for Dr. Sam!"

A rousing cheer drowned out everything Dash wanted to say to Misty.

"Go get your crown—without me." She huffed and wove her way to the exit.

"Wait!" He chased after her, but was waylaid by Misty's brothers. They hogmarched him to the podium and planted him in front of Mayor Tompkins.

"Hey, no running away without your crown," one of them said.

"My sister's playing hard to get," the other said. "You'll be fine."

"No, you don't understand," he said, but it was all to no avail. He couldn't give away his secret and admit to being Dash Weston, so he had to play along and smile and wave to the Christmas revelers.

And so, Dash Weston, the erstwhile Christmas profiteer, was crowned the Christmas Creek Christmas King and made to dance with every filly left in the stables, including Gina Golightly, Hayley Brockman, Angela Wing, Sonja Sexton, and Fianna Tallahan. They chose the slowest cowboy Christmas songs that lasted forever and ever.

And all the while, Dash's hopes were dashed amidst the mistletoe, sawdust, and tinsel all because he'd fallen in love under false pretenses.

Chapter Twenty-Two

Misty tore headlong out of the ballroom, taking long sprinting strides to get as far away from Dash Weston as she could. She pushed through the front door into the biting wind and swirling snow, but not even the weather slowed her down.

Blinded by tears and shooting pains in her heart, she could do nothing but run and run. As long as she kept moving, she wouldn't have to think and to feel. She stomped through the snow-covered fields and stumbled down the hill, not caring where she was going. Somehow she was running faster than she'd ever gone, dashing through the snow in leaps and bounds. She wasn't cold and she practically flew across the forest trails.

Maybe this had all been a bad dream. Maybe she'd wake up and find herself warm and toasty in her bed. Maybe it was the height of summer and she was going skinny-dipping in the swimming hole, daring Merry to join her. Maybe she was speeding around the mountain passes in a convertible, her hair flying in the wind and laughing at the top of her lungs. Maybe she'd hopped onto Santa's sleigh and she was actually soaring through the air behind a team of reindeer and the frost on her face was stardust and she was on her way to heaven where Granny had gone, happy and free with her memory intact, straight to a grand reunion with Grandpa Nick.

"Woof, woof, woof!" A tiny bark nipped at her ear, and instantly, ice invaded her veins. She wasn't flying anywhere. She'd fallen in a pile of snow, and her teeth were chattering and her skin stung with cold.

"Ruff, whirr, grr, ruff." A ball of silver fur and a flash of red silk bounded on her chest. Hot doggy breath steamed in her face.

"Wuh, buh, wes, tee." Her lips were numb, but she held out her arms and hugged the tiny terrier while struggling to open her eyes. Her eyelashes were frozen together, and she was quickly getting frostbitten. She hadn't been running or flying anywhere. She needed to get out of the cold, and fast.

"Wwwoff, wwrrr, grrr," Westie barked, but somehow she understood him. "Follow me."

Stumbling to her feet, she set the terrier down and followed him. He slowed to a trot and kept looking back, so Misty gritted her chattering teeth and put one foot in front of the other.

A tiny cottage appeared down the forested lane, and the lights were on.

Westie sped ahead, barking at the top of his lungs. He hopped up the porch steps and scratched on the cottage door. It opened, and a woman dressed as Mrs. Claus poked her head out.

"Help me!" Misty waved her hand. "I'm cold and lost."

"Oh, my stars!" It was Constanza Zingerman, and somehow she was not at Southside Glen. "Misty Jolly, you come in here right now."

Constanza pulled on her boots and met Misty halfway up the path. Misty was shaking so hard she couldn't walk straight. But leaning on Con's arm, she finally collapsed onto a love seat.

"You'd better get out of those frozen clothes," Con said. "Whatever are you doing out in the cold? Did something happen to Sam?"

"Suh, suh-sam is, is a fuh-fake." Misty managed to enunciate.

"I'm glad Westie found you. He's been here keeping me and my new friend company, and suddenly, he scratched the door, whining to go out. I figured he had to take care of business, but instead of coming back, he dashed through the snow and disappeared." Con kept up the stream of chatter she was famous for.

Misty didn't have time to wonder who Con's new friend was because she called into the kitchen, "Sharky, brew up some hot tea for Miss Jolly. She's practically an icicle."

A round-faced woman with a crown of white curls appeared from the kitchen. "Where's my nephew? I thought the two of you were together. Is he okay?"

"Oh, he's fine." Misty couldn't help the snark. "Crowned Christmas King and dancing the night away with the single and eligible bachelorettes of Christmas Creek."

"Now, now, don't you worry about him," Constanza said. "I'll get you dry clothes and a pair of slippers. Then have tea and tell us all about it."

She handed Misty an old-fashioned Christmas gown with lace in the front. It was velvety and warm. Misty was so very exhausted, so she went into the bedroom and stripped off the frozen saloon dress, stockings, and stiff boots. The fluffy gown felt like heaven along with the fluffy slippers.

Aunt Sharky returned from the kitchen with a teapot and a cup. "You shouldn't be alone right now. Why don't you thaw out in front of the fire with us?"

Misty sat down in front of the toasty fire. Tea sounded good, and when Dash's aunt offered her a platter of gingerbread cookies, Misty graciously accepted.

"I'm sorry to meet you under such circumstances," Sharky said. "You probably guessed I'm Dash's Aunt Sharky. I know him better than anyone, and I have no excuses for him. Westie tells us he's hurt you badly."

"Westie talks to you too?" Misty glanced at the terrier who was cuddling with Constanza. "I thought I was crazy when thoughts popped into my mind."

"He has a way with barks, growls, and whines," Aunt Sharky said. "I don't want you to get freaked out, but he only visits when Dash is in trouble."

"What do you mean, he only visits?" Misty bit into the head of a boy gingerbread cookie.

"If you get close to Dash, you'll know soon enough. When things go well, we never see Westie."

The terrier raised his head and howled, but no thought popped into Misty's mind other than "She thinks she knows me."

"Not going to tell me, are you?" She put her hand out for the dog who licked her fingers. "Are you Dash's guardian angel?"

"Woof, whirr, ruff, woahhwow," Westie said, meaning, "I told Dash to tell you the truth."

"He did, but it's too late. Thanks for caring about him," Misty said. "There's no excuse for what he did to me."

"No, there isn't," Aunt Sharky said. "It's for him to fix this."

Misty didn't want to tell her there was no fixing it. She hated being lied to and furthermore, betrayed. As far as she could tell, she'd been kicked off the Southside project. She wanted no favors from Dash, and she wasn't for sale. No way. No how.

"I'm sorry," Misty said, dabbing at her eyes. "It's been disappointing for all of us, but it *is* Christmas. Let's be grateful we can celebrate the love of God and his gift to mankind."

"Hear, hear," Con said, and the three women toasted each other's teacups. "Merry Christmas. God bless us all."

"It's Christmastime, the best day of the year," Misty said. "A time for hope, for new dreams, and leaving old hurts behind. When you see Dash, let him know I'll keep his secret. Eventually, I'll forgive him, but I don't ever want to see him again and I don't want any favors from him. No recommendations. No promotions. No business deals. No contact. It's over."

Westie jumped on Misty's lap and licked the tears streaming down her face, and thankfully, neither Con or Sharky contradicted her or spoke for Dash and his dastardly deeds.

"Can I keep you?" She hugged the terrier who would be her only link to a love lost before it was rightly found.

"Ruff, whirr, wrrr, woof," the puppy answered, meaning, "I'm yours as long as Dash needs me to be."

* * *

The party was winding down as people headed home to sleep and set out presents for Christmas morn. Dash was on the lookout for Misty, but she was obviously avoiding him. She couldn't possibly have driven away since they'd hitched a ride with the mayor, but the mansion was large and she was probably hiding out until the coast was clear.

"I'm sorry, ladies, but I don't deserve this crown," Dash said to the women who danced and took selfies with him. "I'm an imposter. There's no dentist named Dr. Sam and I really, really need to find Misty before anything happens to her."

"This is unbelievable," Fianna Tallahan said. "My brother's the contractor for Southside Glen and he met you when you first came to town. He said Misty found you in the plane wreck."

"She did, but I'm not a dentist." Dash knew he was close to giving away his secret of being a mystery shopper. "I had a fake ID I use whenever I want to get away from my responsibilities."

"Oh, I get it," Gina said. "I used to have a ton of fake IDs I'd use when I went on vacation. I know the feeling. You want to be someone else and see the world from a different point of view."

"My brother knew you were a fake." Angela narrowed her already narrow eyes. "We don't cotton to fraudsters coming into this town and stealing from us."

"Hold it. I didn't steal anything."

"Ahem." A growly male voice cut in. "You tried to frame me with the misplaced Santa throne. Planting it at my furniture shop. My apprentice saw you sneaking around and reported it to the sheriff."

Dash didn't recognize the dark-haired, dark-eyed fellow who wore a threatening demeanor. "I didn't mean anything other than to save you the trouble of completing the replacement. However, I did pay the invoice, and you can keep the replacement for another party or even use it for the town square Santa."

By now, whoever was left at the party gathered around, since Dash's confession was likely the most interesting bit of gossip left before the stockings were hung and the children hit their pillows with visions of sugar plums and fairies dancing in their dreams.

"Oh dear, you mean we've solved the case of the missing Santa throne?" The mayor's wife fanned her heaving breast. "Didn't I vouch for Chance? Said he would never steal? Completely rehabilitated."

"You're Chance Martin," Dash offered his hand for a shake. "Dash Weston. I apologize for causing you trouble. It was only meant as a publicity stunt."

"You're saying that the theft, the toilet, and then your disappearance was a stunt?" Chance growled, crossing his arms. "Well, it worked for me, too, because my bookings tripled after we discovered the throne. I have orders from all over the country for next Christmas."

"Same here!" Hayley Brockman, the proprietress of the General Store, clapped her hands. "After someone uploaded the video of you bent over a barrel of kibble and Westie playing tug of war with your ankle, I was able to make postcards, T-shirts, mugs, and tote bags of your posterior and sell them online."

"And just so you know." Gina hooked his elbow and bumped his hip. "I uploaded videos of you and Misty gawking at our Christmas from the past displays, and titled them the Nine Lives of Sam Single by cutting and pasting a picture of you inside each of the time periods. And now, a ton of visitors from Southside are booking Christmas dinner and our goose is sold out."

"So, all's well that ends well," Angela declared. "My brother was onto you from the start and from the looks of it, you not only brought prosperity to our tiny town but also snagged our most hyperactive citizen who never slowed down enough to date. Where is she anyway?"

"I have to find her," Dash said. "I don't think she's very happy with me right now."

"She's probably with her family in the kitchen, cleaning up," Sonja said. "Chance and I will take down all of the Western props and be out of your way."

"Same here," Hayley said. "Thanks for the dance and the selfie. I've got to get back to the store and wrap my gifts."

"Dad will need me up bright and early to prep the geese," Gina said.

"Party's still going on at Southside," Fianna said, taking Dash's other arm. "Tally and Lucky said there's dancing and carousing at the saloon through the night, just like in the Gold Rush days when no one slept. Wanna come with me?"

"I'm going to have to beg off, but thanks." He had to find Misty and hope she'd let him explain. No matter how well the project went and how much money rolled in, none of it would mean a red penny if he couldn't make it up to Misty. "Show me the way to the kitchen. I want to help the Jolly family with cleanup."

"Oh, my, a humble chief executive," Mrs. Tompkins said. "I'll be glad to escort you on a tour of this historical mansion. Will you be needing a ride back to the Mill Inn?"

"I'll figure it out when I catch up with Misty, but I thank you and Mayor Tompkins for your hospitality."

Mrs. Tompkins picked up Dash's discarded Christmas King crown and set it over his head. "Wear it proudly. If all goes well at Southside, you have just rejuvenated our town. Merry Christmas to you and all of Weston International."

He thanked her and followed her to the kitchen. Right now, Weston International's bottom line was not at all as important as one Misty Jolly. Crossing his fingers, he was shown into the kitchen.

"Where's Misty?" was his first question when he approached Holly and her crew.

"I thought she was with you," she replied. "Wasn't she with you when you got crowned Christmas King?"

"And you're talking," Misty's mom exclaimed. "Are you over your shock?"

"I must be, but I'm concerned about Misty. She ran out when I told her Sam is a fake. I might as well tell all of you now since you're mostly here." He didn't spot Merry and because he was confused about the Jolly brothers, he wasn't sure they were all accounted for. But the important people, her parents, were present.

"What do you mean Sam is a fake?" Ivy's face whitened. "Misty was so in love with Sam."

"Psst. Don't spill it in front of him," Holly said, narrowing her eyes. "You'd better level with us because if you broke my sister's heart, I'm telling Gordon to dissolve his partnership with you."

"Hey, I thought Misty was playing hard to get," one of the brothers said. "Are you saying you lied to her?"

"Shall we punch you in the nose?" Another brother cocked his fist.

"Guys, guys, simmer down," Mr. Jolly's voice boomed. "Let's have the truth. Who are you and what did you do?"

"Shouldn't we try to find Misty first? She might be in danger."

"Or she's hiding from you." Holly took out her phone and placed a call.

"I'm sorry. I didn't mean to hurt her," Dash said, but no one paid him any attention.

Holly said to the phone, "Got it. I'll tell him. I'm so sorry. Yeah, we'll take care of it. Will you be home for Christmas?"

Her expression darkened as she glared at Dash and she said goodbye.

"Is she okay?" he asked. "Is she safe?"

"She's safely hiding from you." Holly pointed her finger at him. "And she says she'll keep your secret, whatever it is, and she'll eventually forgive you, but that it's over. Don't try and find her. She wants no contact."

"I have to explain," Dash cried. "She doesn't understand. I didn't mean to lie to her. I really couldn't talk after I crash-landed."

"But you had a fake ID," Ivy said. "You let all of us think you're Dr. Sam. You played on our sympathy with the plane crash."

"All of which I'm deeply sorry for." Dash hung his head. "I wouldn't object if you all canceled your investment in Southside Glen and drove me out of town with tar and feathers, but all I want is a chance to heal Misty's heart. I love her more than anything, and I'd gladly give up my entire retail empire for a chance to explain."

"She was firm," Holly said. "She doesn't want to hear any more of your lies."

"How about the truth? Will she hear the truth?" Dash pleaded.

"Let's take a chocolate milk and cookie break," Mrs. Jolly said. "And you try that truth serum on us, okay?"

Ivy locked the kitchen door. "Only Jollys in here. Well, except Misty and Merry are missing, and Mick went with Kitty to Southside."

"We have a quorum." Mr. Jolly guided Dash by the arm and set him on a stool facing the kitchen table. He felt like he was on a dunce chair, but it was what he deserved.

After the Jolly family jury took their seats and started gobbling cookies and quaffing hot chocolate, Dash began at the beginning.

"I can't ask you to keep my secret because I'm willing to lose it all for Misty. I know we had a meeting of our hearts, but she thought I was Sam."

"We'll keep your secret if it doesn't hurt anyone," Mr. Jolly said, lowering his round wire-rimmed glasses. "No more deals. Tell us what happened with my daughter."

"Sam Finnegan is one of my mystery shopper personalities," Dash said. "This is the secret of my family's success at retail. We take our customer experience so seriously that we do the mystery shopping ourselves. It's true I had fake identification cards and credit cards in Sam's name, including a business card and a disguise."

"The gray hair is a disguise?" Holly asked.

"No, I'm prematurely gray. Twenty-nine and going on fifty," he added wryly. "It works well in business because it gives me more authority."

"So your family, including your dad and aunt, are mystery shoppers?" Mr. Jolly asked. "Is that why Gordon says you have shark avatars in all your video conference calls?"

"Yes, and we took a big risk to come in person to Southside Glen. Dad and his girlfriend are still in disguise, but Aunt Sharky held a cooking demonstration at the test kitchen and she's going to take a turn at being Mrs. Claus. We really do want this project to be a success, and we are giving all the credit to Misty, and Gordon, too, but Misty had all the great ideas and not only that, but she is detail oriented and efficient. She knows how to execute her ideas and push every facet of it through to completion. Gordon just waves his hands, and Misty gets it done. I was so impressed I wanted to give her a break, so I called my assistant who's also my sister, Darlene, to take over. I'm afraid Misty took it wrong. She thinks I took her off the project."

"She has a right to be upset," Mrs. Jolly said. "She worked so hard. She deserved to be on the viewing stand with the fireworks and ringing in Christmas."

"I wasn't there either, although Gordon stood in for me," Dash continued. "I only wanted to be with Misty, but when she was worried about Sam being missing, I had to bring Sam back. That's when I met her on the road this afternoon and convinced her to spend the evening with me. She would never have done so if she thought I was Dash Weston."

"Misty is very loyal," Ivy said. "You shouldn't have tried to get her to two-time on Sam."

Holly elbowed her twin and shushed her, then turned to Dash. "Misty never forgets a slight, and you not only lied to her, but you betrayed her. Misty is not a compromiser, so don't get your hopes up. What you've told us is disgusting, and I'm going to clue Gordon in. We've brought the town into debt on the project, and we have to trust our business partners."

"I would never do anything to jeopardize the business," Dash said. "I only want to clear the air about what I did. I hope I can convince Misty to give me another chance and fair warning, I'll do anything to make it up to her. She fell in love with Sam, my mystery shopping persona, and I'm hoping she can forgive the businessman me, Dash Weston."

"Sorry, she wants nothing to do with Dash Weston," Holly's statement had an air of finality, except for one loophole. Misty might not want anything to do with Dash, but maybe the door was open a crack for Sam.

He could do Sam again or be Sam forever. Sam was sweet and innocent. Sam was helpful and supportive. Everyone liked Sam, but no one liked Dash.

Decision made, he thanked the family for listening.

"I've got a lot of work to do, and I know we have one thing in common. We both want Misty to be happy."

"Promise me you won't contact her," Holly said.

"I will respect her wishes not to hear from Dash Weston again." He hopped off the dunce stool. "As for the Southside project, tell Gordon that Misty is back on for Christmas Day and the third episode, beginning with Boxing Day."

No one spoke as Dash walked out of the kitchen, and he felt every one of their disapproving glares stabbing holes into him.

Chapter Twenty-Three

Misty hung up the phone, blinking back tears. Both Constanza and Aunt Sharky looked expectantly at her, but she couldn't meet their hopeful gazes.

"That was my family. They just wanted to know if I'm safe. They want me to go home and celebrate Christmas, but I can't. I just can't. I get the feeling Dash is with them and he's going to try something. I can picture him buttering up my mom and dad and getting them to feel sorry for him. My sister Ivy is a big softie and Merry believes that if a dog likes a guy, then he's okay."

Westie barked, "Woof, ruff, wrr, grr, woof," to say, "I like Sam, but I'm not sure about Dash."

"My thoughts exactly," Misty said to the dog, convinced that Constanza and Aunt Sharky understood him too.

"You're welcome to stay here as long as you want," Constanza said. "Sharky and I are going back to Southside tomorrow. Would you like to come with us?"

"For once in my life, I want to be alone. I mean, I was born with Merry and with plenty of brothers and sisters. I'm running so fast I can't hear myself think, and because we are the Christmas family, we're always putting on a show for the town." She put a hand on her chest. "I'm hurt and I just want to hide out."

Westie nosed her and licked her fingers.

"With you, of course." She kissed the little terrier.

"This is the perfect hiding spot," Constanza said. "I'm tucked away behind the frozen fishing hole and out of sight of the main road."

"You sure Dash won't find me here? He knows where my apartment is," Misty said.

"You'll be safe here, and you'll feel better after a hot bath and a good night's sleep," Constanza said. "My guest room is available, and my granddaughters have left plenty of clothes in the closets. They're on a Christmas cruise, and this old gal gets seasick at the slightest wobble. I would have been alone too had it not been for Southside Glen and me being Mrs. Claus."

Misty gave Constanza a hug. "I'm so glad you're Mrs. Claus. I've always wondered what Mrs. Claus does on Christmas night while Santa's out shimmying down chimneys."

"You're about to find out, sweetie." Con lifted the cover off an old record player and put on a Bing Crosby album. "Sharky, let's break out the deck of cards. You up for gin rummy with rum and gin?"

"Sure, but I need a hot bath first." Misty felt grimy after her trek through the snowy fields.

She left Westie with Con and Sharky while she ran the bathwater to heat it up. The clawfoot tub was cozy and cute. Soon, the bathroom was steamy, and Misty gladly eased her worn out body into the hot water filled with lavender-scented suds.

She put her head on the bath pillow and glanced up. A frosted skylight hovered overhead, and as she watched, she thought she saw words written across the frost.

It was the wee hours of Christmas morn, a time when magical things happened. If she hadn't been running around like crazy every year, she might have closed her eyes and listened for jingling bells and reindeer hooves. It would be her luck to have Santa land on the roof this very moment and write her a message on the skylight. But there was no sound of heavy boots or gliding sleighs—just a gentle swishing like a sweeping broom.

Misty slipped underneath the foamy bubbles and relaxed. What was it Merry had told her? That Gramma Frost rode on shooting stars and wrote messages on frosty windows? That she would grant Christmas wishes? Was the Christmas fortune-teller, Jacklyn Frost, the same as the mythical Gramma Frost Dottie believed in?

The warmth of the bath and the calming scent of the suds relaxed her to the bone, and somewhere, maybe outside, she heard a voice above the rustling sound. It was an older woman's deeper, alto voice, motherly and soothing.

Did Con and Sharky have another visitor?

Misty stared at the frosted skylight above and smiled. The crystals were jagged and sparkled so prettily, forming a heart shape with an arrow threading through it. Maybe it was her imagination or fanciful thinking, but she wondered what fortune Jacklyn Frost would have told her had she given her more time. As usual, she'd been in a rush, and figured the entertainer was only telling her what she wanted to hear. Vague things about magic and romance in the air.

Like the frost pattern spread across the glass, its jagged fingers like crooked Christmas tree branches tracing out a heart.

How pathetic. She was seeing lovey-dovey things everywhere.

She was dozing off when her phone rang.

It had better not be Dastardly Dash. She reached over to turn off the ringer, but the number was unfamiliar. What if it was one of the Christmas Village vendors who needed her help?

She should let it go. Darlene was supposed to handle everything. She was getting the credit, so why should she care?

The ringing stopped but started again. Okay, so she still cared about the Christmas Village project. If it wasn't profitable, the entire town would suffer.

She picked up the call. "Hello? May I help you?"

"Misty, my dear," the same soothing female voice said. "I saw a vision, and I felt compelled to call you. Forgive me if I'm disturbing you."

"Are you right outside my bathroom door?" she asked.

"Oh no, I was at the Gills Mansion watching over my poor, misguided boy."

A shudder traveled down Misty's spine. "Who are you? Have we met?"

"Yes, we have. I'm Jacklyn Frost and you never stopped at my booth for a reading."

"I'm sorry. Things got busy. I hope you're doing well there. How can I help you?"

"I see patterns in the frost. Do you see what I see?" Jacklyn's voice took on the mystical tone of soothsayers. "A heart with an arrow piercing it. The crystals are forming a crack, breaking it into two lobes."

"Are you telling me my romance is kaput?" Misty snapped. "Because I already know it's over. It never happened. I got duped by a man pretending to be someone else, and that's why I'm sitting alone in a bathtub full of bubbles soaking myself into a prune while everyone's partying and waiting for Santa at Southside."

"I still foresee a chance for love," Jacklyn said. "I saw my boy spilling his heart and secrets to a concerned family. He confessed it all to them, and yes, he was wrong for disguising himself. And yet, that sweet, innocent boy who loved everything Christmas was real. He was the child I raised, full of wonder and imagination, a believer in the Christmas spirit and goodwill to man. All this was before his father got custody of him and put that hard-nosed business sense into him. He became a perfectionist, a man with high standards putting his customers and employees first, himself last. But when he fell out of the sky and met you—"

"Please stop," Misty said. "Dash put you up to this, didn't he? How do I know you're who you say you are? And if you are his mother, you're obviously in cahoots with him."

"He doesn't know I'm here. I, too, am a mystery shopper, or in this case, a mystery mom. I watch him from afar because we don't agree on his methods. But when he traipses out to mystery shop, I see Sam, and that's the boy I love. I pray you'll see both sides, his determination to excel and his wish to please the one he loves. Both sides of the same perfectionist self."

"I don't particularly like spies," Misty said. "If you're who you say you are, why are you mystery momming? Why don't you speak to him?"

"I have to assure myself my boy is not taking after his philandering father with his revolving door of mystery mistresses. If I reveal myself, he'd be on his best behavior and I would never know if he was true blue or not."

"So you spy on him and his girlfriends?" Misty hoped she didn't sound like a jealous girlfriend prying. "Not that I care."

"He hasn't had one since college. She turned out to be a real loser. He caught her shoplifting and looting one of our flagship stores. She thought she was in disguise, but so was he." The matronly voice chuckled. "He's been very careful since. Business over pleasure. Staying on the sidelines while his father pushes women on him."

"Yuck, so he's a player like him. No, thank you, Mystery Mom."

Jacklyn clucked her tongue. "Thank God he's nothing like his dad in that sense. He went into dating hibernation. Business only. Profits and loss. Spreadsheets over parties. He's meticulous with the formulas and forecasts. Checking every detail and checking them twice. He wasn't interested in any female until you plucked him out of the wreckage."

"How would you know unless he put you up to telling me?"

"My son and I haven't spoken in years," Jacklyn said. "But I know things. I read them in the frosty window panes, and I've been watching him. You led him through town like a little lamb. I suppose getting hit on the head and having that shock made him speechless and gave him the chance to soak in life to the fullest. I saw the joy and wonder in those clear blue eyes, taking me back to the infant on my lap looking up at the stars and the toddler in my arms petting reindeer. Whatever happens, just understand where he's coming from and be gentle with my boy's heart." She hung up without saying goodbye or Merry Christmas.

Misty shook her head, perplexed. Did Dash put this mystery woman up to it? Was she really Dash's mother or another fanciful setup? Could it be Darlene?

She settled back into the cooling water. Somehow, the bath was no longer relaxing, and when she glanced at the skylight, an electric sizzle caught her breath.

The heart shape was no longer cracked. The crystals had formed, not only healing the one heart, but shadowing it with another one—a double heart pierced through with an arrow.

The swishing sound stopped, and she narrowed her eyes at the clear glass above the cleft of the heart. A shooting star zipped across the night sky, and like she always did, she made a wish.

* * *

Dash bummed a ride back to the Jolly ranch where he picked up his "Dash" clothes and identification cards. Misty's family was politely friendly but he could tell they were disappointed and upset with him.

He texted Gordon who gave him a great report of the fireworks show and the continual twenty-four-hour dance party. *The cash is flowing and the party is hopping. Are you coming down?*

Dash: *You carry on. I've promoted Misty to Chief Marketing Officer of Weston International. I want her front and center for the rest of the events.*

Gordon: *I didn't know she worked for you. Holly tells me she wants nothing to do with you.*

News sure traveled fast in small towns. Dash texted back, *I'm working on it and I won't give up. Give Misty all the accolades and credit for the job. She deserves it. As do you.*

Gordon: *It's about time you gave me some credit. Looks like we'll be making money hand over fist. Come to the party. Heard you won Christmas King, and the Christmas King reigns for only a single day. Better make the most of it.*

Dash: *I will, but I won't be seen. I'd rather remain in the background.*

Gordon: *As Sam Single? Great idea. He's the one everyone wants. In fact, all the single women want dates with him.*

Dash: *Sam Single is retiring. If all goes well, I'll be Mr. Misty by the new year.*

Gordon: *Good luck, Cuck. LOL*

Dash: *Likewise you letting Holly string you along. Merry Christmas.*

After changing out of his Sam outfit, Dash wished the Jolly family a Merry Christmas and called for a taxi. Not wanting to stay in their sight a moment longer, he walked down the long, snowy driveway, past the happy snow family, and stopped in front of the Misty snow woman, with her stick arms and legs in a running position. He untied the red silk cravat from his head and lovingly put it on the snow woman as a cape behind her neck.

"Slow down, Miss Misty, and let me catch you." He blew the Misty snow woman a kiss and wandered down to the arched redwood stump gate to wait for the taxicab.

As luck would have it, Donner's vintage red Cadillac with the surplus of chrome rolled up to a stop right up against his belly. A sparkling red gem was embedded on the forehead of the flying goddess hood ornament.

Dash reached out to touch the gem, but Donner shouted a warning. "That's a ruby from the pirate Jacque Dion's red pineapple. A blessing and a curse. It'll give you what you want the most but take something just as valuable for its price. I wouldn't touch it if I were you."

"I want Misty Jolly most of all, and I don't care what it takes." He tapped the flying goddess's forehead. "I want to love her forever and to have her love me back."

Donner shook his head glumly. "The price will be high. I don't know what it will be, but the red pineapple always extracts its pound of flesh."

"So be it." Dash caressed the ruby's facets. An electric shock zapped him, and he yanked his hand back. Nothing else seemed to happen, so he slid into the Cadillac next to Donner. "It was worth a try. Take me to the Mill Inn. I've had a long night."

"Aye, you're missing the missus."

"I hope to make her my missus," Dash said. "But we're far apart right now. She found out I'm not Sam and she doesn't want anything to do with me."

"You look like Sam to me," Donner said. "When she asked me, I was ready to vouch for you."

"That's where you're wrong. I was only pretending to be Sam and since I couldn't speak, I let Misty do the talking for me."

Donner lifted a brushy gray eyebrow. "Are you wrong in the head? You're the same guy I drove to the Mill Inn. You're just wearing someone else's clothes."

Dash wasn't going to argue with the elderly cab driver. It was obviously late, and everyone was exhausted.

"Santa's out and about tonight." Dash craned his neck to look above the snow-laden trees. "I wonder how high he flies. Do you think he goes into orbit?"

"Maybe. It's a busy night for him. So many toys, so little time."

"I wish he could slow down and smell the roses," Dash said.

"What roses? He's sitting behind the reindeer farts. No wonder he has indigestion come Christmas morn."

For some reason, Dash found Donner to be hilarious. "I never thought about reindeer exhaust. Those cookies he picks up better be worth it."

"They are because they were baked with hope and love."

"Yes, hope, faith, and belief." Dash leaned back and inhaled through his nose, imagining a crackling fire, marshmallows toasting on a stick, chestnuts roasting on an open pan, and Misty in his arms, snuggled on a couch underneath a warm blanket. "I want to spend Christmas night with the one I love."

"Got it." Donner turned the land yacht around with a three-point turn.

"Whoa, wait. Where are you going?" Dash asked, putting his hand on the dashboard.

"Taking you to the one you love," Donner said.

"She doesn't want to hear from me. Doesn't want any contact. I have to respect her wishes."

"Do you want her or not?" Donner sounded impatient. "The red pineapple is trying to help you. Don't worry, you'll pay later."

"I want her, but I don't want anything to backfire," Dash explained. "Her sister made it clear."

Donner slid him a slow wink. "So her sister said, but you didn't hear it from her, did you?"

"By golly, you're right. Holly doesn't like me. It's probably the harsh terms I imposed on Gordon's investment. Any cost overruns come out of his share."

"If you could do it over, knowing what you know now..." Donner trailed off.

"I'd be more charitable," Dash said. "In fact, I'd donate the entire proceeds of this trial run of Christmas Village to Christmas Creek. I'm already donating the animal adoption fees to the rescue shelter, and the clothing bought to decorate snow families goes to the homeless shelter. The tree decorating contest goes to the vocational school."

"Have you announced it yet?"

"Oh, no. I'm doing it anonymously. God says if I announce it to the world, I would have gotten my rewards on earth."

"Darn." Donner snapped his fingers as if he were frustrated. "What else are you going to do?"

"Not telling." Dash's gaze was all over the winter wonderland. "It's gorgeous out here. I just want to sit in front of a large bay window overlooking the town and make wishes."

"Wish away." Donner idled the car in front of a rustic-looking cottage with an old rickety porch. "Here's where you should go."

"It's not the Mill Inn."

"No, but it's your destiny."

Dash reached into his pocket and slipped him a hundred-dollar bill. "Merry Christmas, Donner, my friend, no relation to the party. Go to Southside on me and join in on the all-night dancing at the Last Chance Saloon."

"Merry Christmas to you, son." The old man closed the passenger door and opened the back door. "Hey, ladies, let me guess. The Last Chance Saloon at Southside?"

"Why, yes, how did you know?" Constanza dressed in full Mrs. Claus gear said. She tapped Dash. "Now you know what Mrs. Claus does on Christmas night while Mr. Claus is out delivering gifts."

Dash's Aunt Sharky was dressed as a voluminous green elf wearing a white apron with red reindeer motifs. "Hey, nephew, now you know what Auntie Claus does on Christmas night. We're going gambling, carousing, and partying. Lighting up the town red and green. Good luck."

"Last Chance Saloon, here we go." Constanza threw up a deck of cards, scattering them in the snow.

The two of them were already three or four sheets to the wind, so Dash hugged his aunt and gave her a Christmas kiss. "If you see Dad, tell him I'm resigning from Weston International. He'll understand."

"He might not, but your dear mom would. Why don't you give her a call when this is all over?"

"I will."

"Say 'hi' to Sam for me," Constanza hooted as she got into the Cadillac.

"I will."

He watched until his two guardian aunts were giggling in the back seat and the Cadillac turned around to back out. The tiny gem on the hood goddess twinkled like a red star, burning hope into his heart.

Chapter Twenty-Four

Misty stared out Constanza's window at the scene playing out on the driveway. Rage boiled in her stomach, and steam hissed from her nostrils. Why, the two meddlesome aunties had played a trick on her. They'd agreed to stay in with her and play cards and drink gin and rum. It was supposed to be girls' night without men, but the traitors called Dash and were leaving her alone with him.

Well, Misty wasn't going to let him in. With Westie running circles around the living room, she barricaded the door with a ladder-backed chair.

"Go away," she called out when his footsteps sounded on the creaky porch. "I never want to speak to you again."

"Then come on out and enjoy the frosty air." He knocked on the door. "It's a wondrous night. That magical time of the year. Christmas night and the stars are shining bright. I bet ol' Santa's up there zipping like a shooting star way up in the stratosphere."

Urgggh! Misty groaned at the way Dash ignored her wishes.

"I told you I don't want to talk to you."

"Then don't talk," he said. "Listen to the sounds of Christmas. Sleigh bells in the distance, the hoot of an owl, and tiny feet sneaking down the stairs to peek under the Christmas tree."

What was this man trying to do? He'd hurt her with his lies, and now he was acting like nothing happened? Especially after he set her up with the Jacklyn Frost phone call.

Slick and sneaky. That's what he was.

Still, Misty pressed her ear to the door to listen to the sounds he described, but there was only silence.

Westie nosed her and squeezed himself between Misty and the door. Slowly, she slid to the floor and closed her eyes. What was he doing out on that porch? Was it cold out there? But of course it was. Had he left?

She crept to the window and moved the curtains slowly, not wanting to let him see her. She needn't have worried. Dash was out on a snowbank rolling snowballs.

Had he gone nuts? Shouldn't he be at Christmas Village to supervise the all-night festivities? Gordon had texted her that Dash was promoting her to Chief Marketing Officer, and she had categorically told him no way, no how, no José.

He wasn't going to buy her off so easily after his dastardly deeds, but why was he making a snowman at this time of night?

Misty watched as Dash gathered twigs, fir branches, and little pieces of wood to decorate his snowman. When he finished, he took clothes out of a gunny sack and dressed up the snowman. The Sam Single red-and-white-striped Santa's hat went on the snowman's head. He unwrapped his scarf and tied it around the snowman's neck. The round horn-rimmed glasses went on the snowman's face.

He then turned to a tree and hung the lederhosen, the red-and-white-striped sweater, and the rest of Sam Single's socks and boots like ornaments from the branches. Dancing to a tune only he could hear, he threw snow up in the air and turned around in circles. The expression on his face was of glee and joy, like he was a kid who'd never played in the snow before.

He galloped around the tree and raised his hands toward the full moon above, and what was that? He was yodeling, ho, ho, ho, and a yodeling in the snow, and making whipping motions, going faster and faster, and howling to the moon.

What trick was he playing on her now? Making her believe he was going crazy so she'd speak to him? Misty crossed her arms and jutted her lower lip at his silly acting.

"He's not going to make a fool of me again," she told Westie.

"Woof, roof, yo, yo, yooo," Westie howled, meaning, "No, he's only making a fool out of himself."

"He sure is." Misty pulled the chair from barricading the door to the window so she could sit and watch. "If he thinks I'm going to forgive him, he has another think coming."

"Hoo, woo, whooo," Westie whined, "But didn't you say you'd eventually forgive him?"

"Eventually." Misty couldn't let her heart soften. The man didn't deserve forgiveness. But then, neither did anyone deserve forgiveness from God.

Dash had stopped lassoing and galloping. Now he was collecting pinecones and stacking them in a triangle like bowling pins. Misty had always wanted to go bowling on Christmas, since she was the family champ, but somehow, bowling was not a Christmas activity.

Still, Dash seemed to think it was okay because he rolled himself a nice big snowball. He swung the snowball but it missed by a mile. Misty shook her head at how stupid he looked while Westie barked encouragement with his wet nose pressed against the window.

Dash didn't look back like she expected him to. Instead, he rolled a large snowball, one he had to swing with both hands. The snowball slowed down and barely hit the pinecone at the head pin position.

"Oh, gosh, he's so lame." Misty pulled on a jacket over the pajamas she borrowed from Constanza's closet. She shoved her feet into a pair of boots and charged down the porch. "Gimme the next snowball."

If Dash was surprised, he didn't let on. Neither did he speak to her.

Grrr. She felt like shoving her boot up his backside, but instead, she rolled herself a bowling ball sized snowball, packed it nice and hard. She held it up to her chest, narrowed her eyes, and then took the one, two, three, and four steps of a perfect delivery.

The snowball traveled at the exact arc, hitting the pocket at the exact angle she aimed for. All ten pinecones exploded.

"Strike!" Misty jumped up and down. She held up her hand and received a high five from the dweeb, but no words.

What if he lost his voice again?

Dash tried again and missed by another mile, so Misty waved him to her side to demonstrate how he should roll the snowball. It was harder than a real bowling ball due to the lack of finger holes, but the principle was the same.

He was a fast learner, because after hitting a couple of spares, he, too, busted all the cones off the porch.

"You did it!" she squealed and hugged him before realizing what she was doing.

He hugged her back, and she couldn't help noticing how cold he was.

Before she could hold her tongue, she said, "You have to come in and warm up. I've a fire going."

Westie jumped up and down, begging pets from Dash, so she opened the door and ushered him in. She couldn't very well let him freeze outside. It was only humane, and she would do that for any stray animal.

He rubbed his freezing hands in front of the fire while she went to the kitchen to make hot chocolate. She found big fluffy marshmallows and long skewers, and graham crackers and chocolate bars to make s'mores.

When she returned to the living room, Dash was replacing the record on the record player with an Elvis Presley Christmas album.

"I love the king!" she blurted before remembering she wasn't speaking to him.

He took a crown out of his gunny sack. Smiling, he put it on his head and bowed to her. Of course, out of two contestants between her elder brother Nick and Dash impersonating *Sam*, the mayor had picked the visitor to make him feel better. Didn't mean he deserved to be Christmas King.

Misty crossed her arms and turned her back on him. She wasn't going to let him off easily. He was a liar and could not be trusted. Moreover, he was a Christmas hater who only used Christmas to make money.

But when Elvis the King crooned about a blue Christmas, Misty felt strong arms wrap around her, taking away the blue snowflakes and the blue tears that were always so close to her eyes. She turned in his arms and rested her teary face on his chest, sobbing as he held her. Why did he have to hurt her so? And why was she too weak to recover?

The song segued to "I'll Be Home for Christmas," and of course, Misty felt she should be home with her family. She missed them, and she was never sad on Christmas the way she was tonight. Yet, she didn't move out of Dash's arms. He felt so much like *Sam*, she couldn't tear herself away. Was he tricking her again?

Sam or Dash, whoever he was, he felt like home. He wasn't trying to justify himself and he wasn't arguing for her to give him a chance. He was just holding her and comforting her, the way a friend would, the way a man who loved a woman would.

Dare she reopen her heart?

* * *

As Elvis sang "The Wonderful World of Christmas," Dash felt Misty soften against him. She let him hold her, and they swayed to the slow pace of the song. He hoped she could feel how wondrous Christmas was and that she could open her heart on this holiday of forgiveness and redemption. He wanted to her to feel loved and cherished, and have this Christmas feeling remain in her heart throughout the year.

The bluesy swing of "Merry Christmas Baby" loosened their steps and before he was aware of the change, she'd lifted her face toward him, eyes half-closed and serene. The tears were gone, and her blue eyes were mystical and alluring, like soft diamonds in a blue lake. And suggestively, the song steered his lips toward hers and she let him land.

He kissed her, putting every bit of his soul into it. How he loved this woman who'd slowed down enough for him to catch her. He would stay in this dreamy state forever if it meant living in the paradise of her loving arms. He kissed her Merry Christmas, swinging to the blues and melting her until she was taffy in his hands.

By the time the King sang, "If Every Day is Christmas," Dash found himself snuggled with Misty on the comfy couch in front of the fire. She gazed into his eyes, glowing bright, and a faint smile graced her radiant face. Loving her would make every single day be Christmas, endlessly, and even though Dash had no words for her, he would gift her himself every day and in every way.

It took Westie jumping on them to break the spell.

"Woohoohoo, woooo, waaroooh!" the little dog raised his nose and howled, "Go ahead. Make up, you two. Every day is Christmas if you love each other. Go ahead. Say it."

"I love you," Dash said the only thing that mattered. "I love you more than Christmas, but not by much."

* * *

Misty gazed at the man holding her close. His blue eyes were electric, almost maniacal. He was still the crazy guy who'd dropped out of the sky, despite having shaved off his silver goatee and dyed his hair brown. And yet, he wasn't the same.

He told her again. "I love you, Misty Jolly. Love you with all my heart."

"But who are you?" she asked. "Are you Sam or Dash?"

He made a circle with his thumb and index finger, then he flipped his hand one way with the circle down and then the other way with the circle up.

"Two sides of the same coin? Are you saying you're both Sam and Dash?"

He nodded, his eyes large and serious, almost pleading with her to accept this impossibility. Except it wasn't impossible. Dash had come to Christmas Creek impersonating *Sam* to do market research. He had to have *Sam's* personality to do it in such a convincing manner. He didn't know she would be the first person he met. He hadn't set out to deceive her, had he?

She narrowed her eyes and studied him. Rather than quailing under her gaze, he stared back at her—not in a challenging way, but definitely not backing off.

"So, you have parts of Sam and Dash in you."

"I am Sam, and I am Dash." His voice was firm and strong. "When I'm with you, Sam I am. I love and marvel at your energy and appreciate the beauty and detail in everything you do. Christmas is a wondrous and magical day, and with you, every day is Christmas. When I'm running my business, I'm Dash, but I got in trouble when I tried to mix business with pleasure."

"I don't want to be an either or," Misty said. "I'm really good at business, and when you took me off the Southside project, you acted as if I was only good to be your date, to give you pleasure. That hurt me."

"Then if you'll allow me to mix both with you, I will. As long as you understand some decisions are business and shouldn't interfere with pleasure."

"I can't work for you, Dash Weston. Gordon told me about your job offer, and I can't accept it."

He lowered his gaze and appeared to be strengthening his resolve. Misty strengthened hers too. If he was going to throw away what he just said over business expediency, then he didn't deserve a second, third, or fourth chance.

"I can have both if you'll be my wife." He withdrew his hand from his suit jacket pocket. "Will you marry me, Misty? Asking for both Sam and Dash."

Her heart did a giant cartwheel and tears again glittered in her eyes, from surprise and happiness.

"Dash, you can be yourself. You don't have to be Sam, because I now know you have Sam inside you, and I love all of you. But aren't we rushing into something?"

"Oh no, we're not." He opened the velvet box, exposing a dazzling diamond solitaire, and got down on his knee. "I'm dashing through Christmas to get home for Christmas, for you, Misty."

Jacklyn Frost had said to be gentle with her boy's heart.

She couldn't be so impulsive, and she had to turn him down— but gently.

"I'm sorry, Sam or Dash, I can't give myself up and everything I wanted. Even for you. Even for love."

"Sassy Misty, I'm not asking you to give up anything. There's no limit to what you can do. I just want a little part of you."

"Oh, no, you don't. You want all of it. Admit it. You're an all-or-nothing kind of guy. What if I don't want your job offer?"

"This is a proposal, my dear, not a job offer." His face reddened, but that Sam Single glint twinkled and she knew she'd hit a bullseye. "I'd still marry you, even if you turn down chief of marketing."

Misty might be impulsive. She might jump headlong into a tangled mess. But she wasn't stupid. She was definitely a cupcake and frosting on top kind of girl.

She met those true-blue eyes of his and quirked her lips. "Well, then, Christmas King, I'll marry you, and you're still making me chief of marketing."

"I'm not making you chief," he said, slipping the ring onto her finger definitively, as if he had the last word. "You earned it, and you're going to work your tushie off. Because of your suggestion, you're going to be visiting towns and villages worldwide to find that special quality for each and every one of our Christmas Villages. And I'm going to be at your side, having Christmas year-round."

"What happened to being CEO and running the worldwide empire of Weston International? You can't be sampling Christmas goodies and sipping mulled wine and eggnog all year round."

"I resigned. Dad can choose someone else."

Misty's jaw dropped and she blinked, disbelieving. "You what? You quit? Are you right in the head?"

"I'm asking you to marry me, aren't I?"

Westie growled and whirred, jumping up to put his two cents in. "He's laying his heart out for you. Just answer the question, will you? The suspense is killing me."

Misty scooped up Westie with her right arm and held him still, her gaze locked on Dash.

She grinned wickedly, holding out on him. "On one condition."

"Only one?"

"Yes, and you must agree before I answer you."

He rolled his eyes and winked. "Sure, why not? Can't be worse than the curse of the red pineapple. Go ahead. Spell it out."

"I'm the *only* one who gets to call you Sam."

"Sam I am." And when he kissed her, all Sam-like both sweet and hot, like the Viking berserker who fell out of the sky, she knew she was not only home, but forever living in the wonderful, winsome, and wondrous world of Christmas all year round.

Epilogue

Dash twirled a roll of packing tape around his finger as he stared out the window of his corner office high up in the Weston towers. The sun was setting beyond the bay, and the last of its golden rays highlighted the dark-orange towers of the Golden Gate Bridge.

He'd spent almost half his life up here perched above the fog of San Francisco with a bird's eye view of the city's famous landmarks. But it was time to call it quits, despite what dear old dad thought.

Dash took the family pictures off the shelves and gently wrapped them in bubble wrap. His father schooled him the old-fashioned way. Effective executive leadership: firm and effective with no wiggle room and no shades of gray. Perfection in every aspect of running the business with a visionary insight into customer desires.

Weston International didn't just follow the trends or survey customers. Instead, his job was to create a need, set the pace for the future, and lead the market to their direction with rapid prototyping and immersive test marketing.

He picked up a baseball autographed by a hall of famer and lopped it into a box. Back in the early days, his dad had sweetened the deal of his indentured servitude by taking him to the ball parks, lecturing him about heroes and leaders, and setting the bar. He'd worshipped his dad, but when his parents' acrimonious divorce hit the courts, he'd been forced to take sides. Mom wanted him to cultivate his creative side, to be a thinker and not a doer. Dad, well, he charged ahead at full steam and took no prisoners. So, his personal life was less than exemplary, but when looking for a brain surgeon, what did it matter if he'd been married several times?

The door to his office flew open with a whoosh, followed by dear old Dad who never bothered to knock.

"I refuse to take your resignation." Marching to the boxes, he upended the one with the family pictures. "Put everything back. We've got a year of expansion coming up. Your work at Christmas Creek made the front page of the Journal, and communities worldwide are vying for us to develop comparable Christmas Villages. I need you to run the numbers tonight and choose the top ten locations and business partners to work with. I'm making an announcement tomorrow."

"You know my engagement party is tonight. Have Darlene do the deals." Dash picked up the pictures that his father poured onto the carpet. "I'm not changing my mind."

"Has that mother of yours bewitched you? Or is it that Misty Jolly?"

"Dad, we've been over this." He flipped the lid of his laptop open and brought up a spreadsheet. "I can no longer make sense of these numbers. They're reversing themselves on me."

"Bull. You're making excuses. You don't develop learning disabilities as an adult. But even so, go to the doctor and get evaluated. It might be a remnant of the shock you suffered. Or you're getting lazy on me."

"I'm getting engaged is what I'm doing." Dash decided it wasn't worth packing the rest of the boxes. He stuffed the photos and the baseball back into the box and carried it to the door.

"Don't walk out on me."

"I'm not walking out," he said, softening. "I chose you when you made me choose between you and mom. I learned everything I know at your feet, but so did Darlene. She's got the drive and the fire in her belly. I just want to create, to make art, to immerse myself with these new communities, to get to know the people and their traditions, and yes, I'll still work for you to design these Christmas Villages. But I can't do numbers anymore, whether you believe me or not."

It was the pound of flesh the red pineapple took, but his realistic father would poo-poo it as yet another delusion or flight of fancy, much like he'd denigrated the stories he learned at his mother's knee.

"I'll have a word with your mother," Dad snapped.

"No, you won't. You've kept me from speaking to her half my life. There's nothing you can say to her that'll make me change my mind." He patted his father on the back. "Be a good sport and be at the Baytop Lounge. Party starts at ten and lasts all night and into the new year. Open bar for all."

"What? Did you run the numbers? How many people?"

"As many as the lounge can take."

"Aren't you going overbudget on this?" Dad asked, sputtering with disapproval.

"Nope. I don't have a budget." Dash shut his laptop. "Can't read spreadsheets anymore, remember?"

* * *

Misty tried not to gawk from the window of the limousine as she and her family pulled up to the base of Reed Tower, the tallest building in San Francisco. The Westons had bought out the entire Baytop Lounge for her and Dash's engagement party but was also allowing patrons and tourists to ring in the New Year at the same time.

"I told you no one would be wearing a costume." Misty nudged her sister, Ivy, who'd wanted to appear as a New Year's fairy complete with glittery gown and a pair of gossamer wings. She'd ended up toning it down to the gown only with a white feathered boa and long satiny gloves.

Meanwhile, Holly wore a fiery red and orange cocktail dress that accentuated her fuller figure while Merry and Kitty were more conservative with smart figure-hugging dresses that fell below their knees.

Misty chose a classic off-shouldered A-line dress with a pleated flared skirt and a crisscrossing V-neck. A delicate diamond necklace with a centerpiece pear-shaped blue diamond sat on her breast, and she wore a matching pair of blue-diamond teardrop earrings.

"No costumes here," Mom remarked. "Most everyone is dressed similarly. Why all the black for New Year's Eve?"

"City folk," Dad said, although all the men in their party wore black tuxes. "Lack of imagination. Or it's the trend."

"I hope we're not overdressed," Gordon said. "Of course, Mr. Weston senior will be at the party. Misty, you checked with Dash on making the introductions, right?"

"Of course I did. Dash says his father is looking forward to meeting you. Seems he wants another protégé now that Dash is resigning."

"No, heaven forbid," Holly said. "Gordon's already too busy as it is."

The limousine driver put the car in park in front of the red carpet and opened the door.

"What are we supposed to do?" Mom whispered to Misty. "Walk across the red carpet?"

"Just go in groups of two or three and act like you're a movie star. Then take pictures in front of the Weston banner."

"I'm afraid I'll trip and make a splat," Ivy said. "Brad, you'll hold on to me, won't you?"

Her sheriff boyfriend, who looked extremely uncomfortable in his suit, grunted. But Misty was glad her siblings and their plus ones were present.

Misty picked up Westie and tucked him into a satin sling looped over one shoulder. Instead of a bright-red cape, he was tastefully attired with a sky-blue silk cravat and a diamond-studded collar.

"Thank you, everyone, for coming," Misty said, trying not to be teary-eyed as they got out of the limousine. Her smile brightened as Dash hurried toward them along with his mother, Jacklyn Frost.

The last time Misty saw her, she was in her snowflake and stars costume, but tonight, she was ravishing in a silver sequin gown, with sparkling jewelry splattered across her décolletage.

"Misty, my dear daughter to be." She reached over and air-kissed her while Westie got in a few licks of her face. "And how wonderful to meet your family. Dash, would you be a dear and introduce us?"

After introductions, Dash offered Misty his right arm and his mother his left, and they survived the paparazzi and the red carpet with no mishaps.

The ride up the golden elevators was dizzying fast, and Misty was sure her ears would pop with the altitude. Westie was strangely quiet, and she wondered why he wasn't commenting. Instead, he acted very dog-like with his nose busy and his tongue lolling.

The party stepped out into the glass-enclosed three-hundred-sixty-degree rotating bar and exhaled a collective "Wow."

The Baytop Lounge was opulently decorated with giant glittery disco balls rotating and spreading beams of multicolored light. Mirrors and windows abounded, especially the floor-to-ceiling ones along the perimeter of the rotating bar. Beyond the windows, the lights of the Golden Gate bridge and the skyscrapers and city skyline filled the panoramic view. Throngs of people danced and celebrated all around them, and an endless stream of well-wishers congratulated her and Dash.

Misty couldn't get enough of the sights and sounds, the press of people surrounding her, the free flow of drinks and finger foods, and the gay party atmosphere. It was as if the entire city turned out to count down the old year and ring in the new.

"Are your father and sister here?" Misty asked Dash during a break in the music.

Dash put his finger to his lips. "They're here incognito. So is Aunt Sharky and our newest mystery shopping recruit, Aunt Con. They're in deep disguise, but rest assured, they're wishing us well. They just can't blow their covers."

"Does that mean you'll never mystery shop again now that your cover is blown?"

"What cover do you mean?" Dash tented his eyebrows as if he was innocent. He pulled on Sam's horn-rimmed glasses and winked.

Taking her left hand, he raised it to show everyone her ring. Looking each member in the eyes, he announced, "I hereby present to you, the future Mr. and Mrs. Sam Frost. There was no Dash Weston Jr. other than on the annual reports and in the company directory."

"I can attest to that, my dear S.F." Jacklyn Frost produced an embossed birth certificate which read, *Sam Frost. Mother: Jacklyn Frost. Father: Dash Weston.* "We were never married. It was all for show, including the divorce. This time, Sam, you chose wisely."

"You mean, I'm going to be Misty Frost?" Her yelp was drowned out by the rowdy crowd counting down to the flashing numbers projected onto the windows.

"Five, four, three, two, one!"

Sam locked his lips over hers, kissing her into the New Year, and Westie howled, "Waaahhhhhoooo!" to the orchestra striking up "Auld Lang Syne."

And for once, Misty Jolly wasn't in a hurry to go anywhere.

~ The End ~

* * *

Thanks for reading Misty and Dash/Sam's mistaken identity romance, with a bit of help from Westie, the super terrier! I hope you enjoyed **Dashing Through Christmas**, and that you'll give it a great review so that others can know what it's all about. I really appreciate it.

* * *

Misty's twin sister, Merry, has her own romance brewing after she finds a lost child near a frozen creek. You can read all about it in **Dottie's Christmas Wish.**

Acknowledgements

Thank you for reading Misty and Sam/Dash's mad dash through Christmas while finding love where they least expected. I hope your Christmas season is filled with family, fun, and festivity but also moments of quiet, peace, and the comforts of home.

If you liked this story, please do tell your friends about me and/or write a review to let others in on this magical place called Christmas Creek.

A grateful thank you to my first reader, Amber McCallister, and my editor, Kimberly Dawn for always putting my work first. I also appreciate each and every reader for dashing through the holiday season along with me.

Merry Christmas!

About the Author

Rachelle Ayala is a *USA Today* bestselling author of dramatic romantic suspense and humorous contemporary romances. She is the winner of multiple awards, including the 2015 Angie Ovation Award for best Multicultural Romance with *Knowing Vera*, the 2015 Readers' Favorite Gold Award for *A Father for Christmas*, the 2016 Readers' Favorite Gold Award for *Christmas Stray*, the 2016 Readers' Favorite Finalist for *A Pet for Christmas*, and the 2017 Readers' Favorite Gold Award for *Playing for the Save*.

For updates and a surprise free book, sign up for Rachelle's newsletter at:
http://smarturl.it/RachAyala

Check out her website for a list of books and readers' guide:
http://rachelleayala.net

To chat and read new works in progress, join her Reader's Club at:
http://www.facebook.com/groups/ClubRachelleAyala/

Printed in Great Britain
by Amazon

86959935R00113